The carton sitting on the floor of my living room was too tempting to set aside. I lifted it onto the coffee table and pulled open the four flaps that had been neatly folded into each other.

On top was a small white leather photograph album that said OUR WEDDING in gold on the cover. The pages were plastic envelopes and each one was filled, front and back. The first few pages showed a bride dressing: a white, street-length dress going over her head, her carefully coifed hair being brushed into place by a man with a brush and a very dedicated expression, mascara being applied in a mirror shot that focused on her reflection.

Sandy had not exaggerated. Natalie was beautiful, with reddish brown hair and a smile as lovely as it was natural. The dress was simple and elegant, the short veil, when she finally had it on, very fine looking. There were a few snapshots also of the ceremony, which took place under the traditional canopy of a Jewish wedding. In one picture, Sandy was stamping on a white package on the floor, probably the glass he was to break to assure good luck to the couple. The luck hadn't lasted very long. . . .

By Lee Harris
Published by Fawcett Books:

THE GOOD FRIDAY MURDER
THE YOM KIPPUR MURDER
THE CHRISTENING DAY MURDER
THE ST. PATRICK'S DAY MURDER
THE CHRISTMAS NIGHT MURDER
THE THANKSGIVING DAY MURDER

Books published by The Ballantine Publishing Group
are available at quantity discounts on bulk purchases
for premium, educational, fund-raising, and special
sales use. For details, please call 1-800-733-3000.

THE
THANKSGIVING
DAY MURDER

Lee Harris

FAWCETT GOLD MEDAL • NEW YORK

A Fawcett Gold Medal Book
Published by Ballantine Books
Copyright © 1995 by Lee Harris

Library of Congress Catalog Card Number: 95-90427

ISBN 0-449-14923-4

Manufactured in the United States of America

First Edition: November 1995

10 9 8 7 6 5 4 3

The author wishes to thank
Ana M. Soler, James L. V. Wegman,
Alan E. Baker, C.P.A.,
Matthew G. Saltarelli, M.D.,
Walter Johnson,
and Karen Shalom of the School of Art, Old Church
Cultural Center, Demarest, New Jersey
for their patience, cooperation, and invaluable information.

For Frank Randall
who's seen more parades than I have

There is one day that is ours. There is one day when all we Americans who are not self-made go back to the old home to eat saleratus biscuits and marvel how much nearer to the porch the old pump looks than it used to. Bless the day. . . . Thanksgiving Day . . . is the one day that is purely American.

—O. Henry (1862–1910)
The Trimmed Lamp
Two Thanksgiving Day Gentlemen

1

I drove my cousin Gene back to the residence for retarded adults after mass that very cold Sunday morning. On many Sundays he joins us for dinner or the afternoon or I join him at Greenwillow while Jack studies, but on that Sunday Jack and I were invited to our friend and neighbor Melanie Gross's house just down and across the street from us for a Sunday brunch. When I got home from Greenwillow, I changed my clothes. I am still old-fashioned enough to dress for church, but Mel had said to come casual and I put on a pair of wool pants and a white cotton blouse, taking along a sweater I probably wouldn't need in Mel's always warm house.

Jack, my husband of half a year, a detective sergeant in the NYPD by day and a law student by night, quickly took his "good" clothes off and got comfortable. At five to eleven, we locked the house and walked down the block.

"Who's coming?" he asked as we neared the Grosses' driveway.

"Mel said a mélange—friends, neighbors, even some relatives."

"What's the occasion?"

I laughed. "It's Sunday and Mel likes to invite people and cook for them."

"Oh, that kind of occasion."

"There's a New Jersey car. I think that's the relatives."

"Looks like snow."

1

"Well, we don't have a long ride home."

"Let's have a fire tonight. That firewood looks really great, good and hard and well seasoned."

I slipped my arm around his waist, feeling the pleasure of marriage as once, in another way, I experienced the pleasure of living in a convent among wonderful women who are still my friends and will be forever.

The door opened as we reached it and Melanie wrapped her arms around me as though we hadn't seen each other in years.

"Welcome! Good to see you. Jack, I hope you're hungry."

"When am I not hungry? Hi, Mel."

Inside, several people, none of whom I knew, had already arrived and Mel took us around, introducing as we went. Her dining room table was set extravagantly and her family room was set up with the most beautiful buffet I had seen executed by a nonprofessional. (Jack's sister is a caterer, so I've seen some professional ones.) Not for the first time, I stood shaking my head in awe.

"How do you do it, Mel?"

"You know me. I like to keep busy."

"It looks fantastic," Jack said.

"Well, I learned a thing or two from your sister at your wedding. I hope she doesn't mind my picking her brain. She was very generous with her secrets, Jack."

His sister is a very generous person. Before we were married, she often gave Jack samples and leftovers, and though we're farther from her now, she always manages to have some tantalizing food wrapped up for us in foil at the end of a visit.

"Why don't we sit down," Mel said.

"Why don't we have some food first," Hal, her husband, suggested to laughter.

"Good idea. Come on, kids, you first and then upstairs with you."

The two Gross children, both very young, had ear-to-ear smiles. With help from their parents and baby-sitter, they loaded enough food on their plates for twice their number at twice their size and then ran off. It was open season for adults.

Jack sat next to Hal, a lawyer who was strongly encouraging of Jack's pursuit of a degree, and I sat on the other side of the table between Mel's college roommate and maid of honor and her husband.

"Mel told me you're an ex-nun," Rachel said. "Do you mind talking about it?"

"Of course not."

"You look too young to have been a nun for long."

"I spent fifteen years in the convent. I went in at fifteen. There were family problems—I'd been orphaned—and St. Stephen's was kind enough to take me, although that's a lot younger than they accept novices."

"Incredible. You spent fifteen years in a convent?"

"Except for one when I got my master's. They were wonderful years."

"I guess what I'm curious about is what you did, how you spent your time."

"Most of it in a very ordinary way. After I finished my education, I taught at the college connected with the convent."

"Just as if you were a lay teacher?"

"Exactly. Of course, I turned my salary, such as it was, over to the convent and they gave me back what I needed to live on. There are nuns in some convents who hold regular jobs outside the convent, working for the telephone company or some other company and earning a regular salary. They come home to the convent at night, and on payday the convent gives them their carfare for the week, enough money for lunches, and anything else they might need."

"So the convent comes out ahead."

I smiled at her. "So does the nun. She has all the advantages of being part of a religious community. She participates in morning and evening prayers, she's able to join activities that take place on Saturdays, go to retreats. There are many wonderful benefits to being part of a convent."

"You really loved it, didn't you?" she said, sounding partly surprised and partly admiring.

"Very much."

"And then you left."

Tactfully, she didn't ask why. "I felt I had given all I could to St. Stephen's, that I had more to give and this was where I could do it."

"You sound amazing."

I laughed again. "I'm probably the least amazing person you've ever met. I teach a course in poetry at a college not too far from here and I do some work for a lawyer in New York who's become a friend of mine. Right now I'm trying to build a good, strong marriage. I'm friends with the convent, I visit there; in fact, we spent Christmas with them."

"Your husband, too?"

"Both of us, yes. But I stayed on for a few extra days."

"Oh, Mel told me about that. There was a murder, wasn't there?"

"Unfortunately. It was very sad."

"You should talk to Mel's uncle."

"Oh?"

"There's something very weird in his life."

"I'm not much of an expert on weird things," I said, hoping to avoid being drawn into a family problem. "Do you live around here?"

She switched easily to talking about her home and her family, and after a moment, her husband joined in on my other side. They had suggestions on landscaping that I took note of. One of the things Jack and I wanted to do was increase the greenery on our property. Eventually it was time for dessert and coffee, for moving to chairs and sofas in the family and living rooms, for talking to other people and enjoying their conversation.

The afternoon passed so quickly, I was surprised to find it was after three and the first guests were getting their coats. I looked around to see whether Jack was ready to leave. Weekends are mainly for studying now that he goes to law school at night, but he seemed happily engaged talking to Rachel and her husband.

"Mrs. Brooks?"

I turned to see a tall, good-looking man about fifty standing next to me with a drink in his hand. His dark hair was newly graying, his eyes soft and gray-green, warm and easy. He was wearing a sporty shirt that struck me as expensive, the kind of appraisal I don't often make. "I'm Chris," I said. "Christine Bennett Brooks. I don't think we've met."

"I'm Sandy Gordon, part of Melanie's diverse, unmanageable family."

"Are you the diverse part or the unmanageable?" I asked, amused at the characterization.

"Probably both. Can we talk?"

"Sure."

He led the way to the dining room, where the table, still covered with most of the dishes of the feast, was empty of people. Sandy Gordon pulled out a chair for me at what had been the head of the table, and he sat along the side so we faced each other.

"Mel's told me a lot about you."

"We've been neighbors for a year and a half and friends for most of that time."

"I was talking to your husband earlier. He sounds smarter than most of the cops I've met."

It's one of the things that makes me bristle. "Jack isn't the only smart person in the police department. They have a tough job, and sometimes the best they can do is follow the rules and procedures and not act as smart as they really are."

He raised his hands as though to ward off a blow. "Forgive me, I didn't mean anything insulting. I like your husband. I admire anyone who goes back to school when he has a full-time job and the usual responsibilities of life. I need your help, Chris. You may not think it to look at me, but I am a desperate man with a problem that no one has been able to solve, and believe me, I have tried to solve it."

People's lives are full of unsolvable problems. You don't need to be religious to know that. Trouble hits all people equally, from what I've seen. And I feel for someone who has suffered misfortune. "Of course I'll help you if I can," I said.

At that moment my idea of what his problem might be was so far from the reality I was about to hear that we were almost in separate worlds. I imagined something to do with the church, with a convent, with a person having religious difficulty. So when he started to explain, when the impact of his profound calamity struck me, I hardly knew what to say.

"I was married two years ago. It wasn't my first marriage, but it was everything I ever dreamed of. She was younger than I, a dozen years or so, it doesn't matter, very beautiful, a little crazy, a little wild, very loving, very happy to be with me. We did a lot of things together. She would come into the city in the evening and we'd have dinner together, go to the theater, listen to music. I don't travel much in my business, but when I did, she came with me. In the winter we skied, in the summer we hiked in the mountains. We were happy and well suited to one another.

"I had told her before we married that I didn't want any children. I have two from my first marriage and I was already well into my forties when I met Natalie. I didn't want to start over at fifty with a baby who would graduate college after I was retired. But I changed. She was so young and energetic and full of life, I told her I wouldn't mind. I said if she wanted a child, it was fine with me. It was her decision. Whatever happened, I would be happy."

I started feeling uncomfortable, almost a little sick. I could hear tragedy in every word he spoke. Whatever was coming, I didn't want to hear it and I knew I had to.

"You OK?" he asked.

"Yes."

"Like something to drink?"

"No. Go on."

"I'll be right back. Don't go away." He left the table and went to the kitchen, returning in a minute with a tall glass of orange juice.

I drank it thirstily. "Go on, please."

"A year ago last November we made plans to go to the Caribbean for Christmas. I told Natalie to go out and buy herself some cruise clothes. She came home with the most gorgeous stuff I've ever seen, bathing suits and sandals and colorful dresses to wear for dinner and dancing. And she was so excited, like a little kid. She modeled them for me and she looked great in everything. I can't describe to you how happy she was.

"We were invited here for Thanksgiving dinner. You probably know what a great cook Mel is, and for one reason or another, she hadn't met Natalie yet. So when she invited us, we accepted. Dinner wasn't till afternoon, of course, and we decided to go to the Macy's parade first. We got up early, drove into the city, parked up near Columbia, and took a cab down to the Seventies, near where the parade starts. We stood on the west side of Central Park West, the side where the apartment houses are, and watched the bands and jugglers and floats and balloons come down the street."

Now, as he spoke, the strangest thing happened to me. As if from the deepest part of my memory, I saw the parade. I was with my father, and we, too, stood on the street in front of a large apartment house, surrounded by throngs, adults and children, vendors selling food and balloons. How had I forgotten? How could I have let such a wonderful memory slip away into obscurity?

"We didn't eat anything," Sandy Gordon went on, oblivious of my own personal involvement in the day, "because we were eating later. But I remember seeing a balloon man come down the street with a whole bouquet of colored balloons, and as he passed us, I saw Natalie look after him. Then she said, 'I'm going to get one.' I told her I'd get one for her, but she was already on her way. The balloon man had turned the corner toward Columbus Avenue, and I just barely saw her turn the corner, too, and go after him." He stopped and took a breath. "I never saw her again."

I didn't know what to say. As he had spoken I had seen the image of the beautiful young woman, and I could feel her vitality in his words. I sensed she had the kind of good looks that needed no makeup, the kind of personality that sparkled in an empty room. He had conveyed her essence to me so completely that I believed I could pick her out in a crowd.

"I'm so sorry," I said. "It's so hard to believe. What a terrible blow it must have been, what a horror."

"Horror is the word. I suppose it took me several minutes to realize she should have come back. One of the parade balloons was going by, Babar, I think, and I was looking up at it and then I looked around and she wasn't there and I got a little anxious. I pushed my way through the crowd to the corner and went around to Seventy-fourth Street. It was empty. There were no people, there was no balloon man, there was no Natalie. I looked around, I looked up and there was one lone balloon rising into the sky. I was scared to death. I called her, I ran toward Columbus Avenue, looking in doorways, crossed the street and came back, told myself to calm down, that I'd just missed her; maybe she'd crossed Seventy-fourth to buy her balloon and as she was coming back to me, I was looking for her. I went back to where I was pretty sure we'd been standing, but I didn't find her. The long and short of it is, I never saw her again."

I could feel his fear. I could understand the terror of losing someone, a beautiful woman on a street in New York. "You reported it to the police," I said.

"I waited for the parade to end, telling myself I was overreacting, that when the streets cleared, she would turn up. It was a long time before Santa Claus rolled down Central Park West with the street cleaners right in his wake. As soon as he passes, the crowd disperses. Some of them go to one of the nearby subway stations on CPW, some of them go over to Broadway and pick up a subway or bus or cab over there. I stood in the street till it was empty, Chris, till the last kid and the last parent disappeared. Then I found a cop and told him my story."

That, of course, was why he didn't think much of cops. Where adults are concerned, a missing person isn't treated the way homicide is. Homicide is concrete, visible, amenable to scientific investigation. A missing person is the absence of all of the above. The police have only the word of an allegedly interested party that someone allegedly disappeared at an alleged time and place. In some cases the police must surely ask themselves whether the missing person ever existed. And adults are different from children; they are responsible to themselves and they have no obligation, certainly no legal one, to remain in a place or with a person if they don't feel like it. The police may look out for the person, but even if they find him, they have no legal right to bring him back. It is a loss like no other.

"And nothing ever turned up," I said.

"Nothing. In fact, the little I learned only made things worse. Although Natalie was in her thirties, her life seemed to begin a few years before I met her. Before that, there's nothing, no family, no history, no job. I'm not sure anymore who the girl I married was, where she came from, even whether she was married before she met me." He opened his hands. "I've come up empty, emptier than before. I'm torn up over this, the loss, the wondering what happened to her. Sometimes I dream of that balloon man walking by us. I see him coming and I see him going and I know he's the messenger of the greatest loss in my life. And I wonder, why didn't I know when I saw him coming down the street that he carried that terrible message?"

In my mind I could see it, the almost invisible man beneath all the balloons inflated with helium reaching for the sky, children with balloons tied to their wrists to keep them from escaping. How sad that such a beautiful, colorful image meant something so evil to this poor man.

"Was she pregnant?" I asked finally.

"I don't know." He answered quickly, as though he knew the answer to every question an investigator might ask, and he probably did.

"I'm so terribly sorry for your loss," I said.

"I want to hire you, Chris."

I must have looked startled because he said, "Don't say anything. Just listen for a minute. I have looked for her. I have had a private detective look for her. I have played games with the police while they supposedly looked for her. She's gone. She's nowhere. She turned a corner and disappeared off the face of the earth. Whether she's dead or alive, I must know. I can't function anymore. I can't move forward and I've never been able to stand still. You have to help me."

"I'm not a private detective, Sandy. I can't accept money to investigate her disappearance, and frankly, I wouldn't know how to start." I felt at a total loss. A woman turns a corner and disappears off the face of the earth. Where do you begin?

"Don't turn me down so quickly. I know you're not licensed. I'm not asking you to do anything that isn't legal. Forget the money; we can talk about that later. If you'd like me to give a donation to your favorite charity, I'm more than happy to do that. I'll pay your expenses. I'll give you every picture of her that I have, every scrap of writing that I've been able to dig up. I have lists of her favorite foods, her favorite perfume, expressions she always used. And I have a few things that may be useful that I didn't have when I hired the detective. It's all yours. My life is an open book; I'll answer any question you have with absolute truth. Just don't turn me down."

My heart really went out to him, but this was so different from the other cases I'd worked on, cases in which I had a personal interest, in which there was some physical evidence, something to go on. What was there here? A balloon floating skyward, an empty street, a crowd of people who had noticed nothing.

"Chris?"

I turned to see Jack standing in the doorway, his coat on and mine over his arm. "Jack. Sandy and I were just talking."

"You want to stay? I can make it home alone." He gave me a smile.

"Why don't you go?" Sandy said to me. "I'll be in touch. Just think about it."

I felt troubled and uncertain. "Fine." I offered my hand and we shook.

"Nice meeting you, Jack," Sandy said, standing as I did. "So long, folks."

"You look like you're not all here," Jack said as he helped me on with my coat.

"Let's talk about it outside."

We found Mel and Hal and said our good-byes, Mel pressing a CARE package on me as we left.

"Thank goodness for Mel," Jack said as we stepped into the cold, dark winter late afternoon. "At least I'm off the hook for cooking dinner."

2

"He get you shook up about something?"

"He told me a terrible story, but there's something else shaking me up. You talked to him, didn't you?"

"For kind of a long time after lunch. Seems like a nice enough guy."

"He said he was related to Melanie."

"He's her uncle."

That surprised me. "He looks kind of young to be her uncle."

"Said he was her mother's kid brother, a lot younger than her mother."

"Mel's old roommate mentioned him during brunch. She said he had a weird story to tell. I had no idea this was the man and that was the story."

Jack took his key out of his pocket and we turned up the front walk. The snow had been shoveled away and the shrubs we had planted in the fall looked healthy and green in spite of the cold. "Do I get to hear the story?"

"His wife disappeared during the Thanksgiving Day parade the year before last."

"That is weird."

"Without a trace. She turned a corner to buy a balloon and he never saw her again."

We walked inside and I went to turn the heat up as Jack closed and locked the front door.

"Feel like a fire?" he called.

"You bet," I called back. "Want something to drink?"

"Maybe some coffee. I tried some of Hal's special single-malt Scotch, and if I have anything else, I won't be able to study."

I put on a pot and rubbed my hands together, happy for the fire I could already smell. The heat would take time, but the fire was instantaneous. Jack had already talked about the possibility of putting a wood-burning stove in the fireplace and heating the downstairs with it. It struck me as a good idea with a downside; I love the look of a fire. A good fire is more interesting than a television screen. Anyway, it was a thought for the future.

When I carried in the carafe, the living room was warm and fragrant with the woody smells I love so much.

"That smells good," Jack said, referring to the coffee.

"So does that." I nodded toward the fire.

"You know me. Nothing smells as good to a cop as fresh coffee."

I leaned over and kissed his cheek, then took the carafe back to the kitchen. When we were sipping in front of the fire, I told Jack what I remembered of Sandy Gordon's story.

"Those things are very tough," Jack said when he'd heard the whole thing. "I have to believe there's a large possibility this woman planned her disappearance right down to saying she was going for a balloon."

"He was at great pains to tell me how happy they were together."

"They're always happy together, Chris. And then one day one of them leaves and the other one can't believe it. I wish I could tell you this was unique, that I'd never heard anything like it before."

"What usually happens?"

"Sometimes the missing person never shows up. The case is kept open, but it's not very active. Sometimes we find a body. That's when we know it was really a case of kidnapping, assault, rape, whatever. It's also possible, of course, that the spouse who reports the disappearance is the killer."

"I can't believe that."

"Believe it."

"Not in this case."

"I tend to agree with you. This guy doesn't strike me as a killer, but you never know. You don't know what really went on between them, what he found out from her or about her before the Thanksgiving Day parade. What he told you was his well-thought-out story."

"But he went to the parade with her and reported her disappearance to the police." I felt myself arguing Sandy's point of view.

"In my scenario, he went to the parade alone. She was already dead and buried when he got to the parade. Who's ever going to remember this guy after the parade's over? He told you Seventy-fourth Street. Maybe he was at Fifty-ninth and walked up to Seventy-fourth to report her missing."

It is a constant amazement to me that my husband, who has a sense of humor, an easygoing personality, and is full of life and love, has this other side. It isn't a dark side of him; it's a knowledge of the dark side of life. He's seen it, he's heard about it, in many cases he's experienced it. Something in me always wants to argue with him, but I know he speaks from direct knowledge.

"Then why would he try to hire me?" I said finally. "He's already done enough to prove to the world that he really wants her back. He hired a private detective after it happened."

"Maybe Melanie suggested it."

It was possible, of course.

"Chris, I'm not suggesting that this very nice guy that we met at a Sunday brunch is a killer. I'm just giving you a scenario. Do I think he killed his wife? No."

"So either she decided to skip out of this marriage and this life or someone grabbed her on Seventy-fourth Street and took her away."

"And since Sandy has discovered that this woman's past is a little unclear, to say the least, either one of those things could have happened. Maybe she decided to go back to the other life."

"Maybe someone from the other life decided to make her pay for something she did in the other life."

"And maybe," Jack said as he got up to get the carafe, "somebody saw a gorgeous woman alone, buying a balloon, and he grabbed her and spirited her away."

"Then she's dead," I said.

He came back with the coffee. "I'd guess that, unless Mrs. Gordon initiated her own disappearance, that was the outcome."

"He wants to pay me to find out what happened. I told him that was impossible."

Jack didn't say anything. He's always been cautious commenting on certain kinds of things, but I've noticed that recently, since he started his second year of law school, his caution has increased, as though he sees himself differently, as though perhaps it's wiser to say nothing than to say something that might be interpreted in the wrong way.

"But I feel sorry for him," I added.

"You know I'm very proud of you," he said, and I knew something else was coming. "You've done this kind of thing so well, I guess you've gotten a well-earned reputation. But this is really different."

"I know. It's why I'm not getting involved."

"In the other cases, you had a personal interest in the victim. This is more like a police case, something a detective catches by chance."

"I'm not doing it, Jack."

"But it's affected you. I sense that you've involved yourself in this just by listening to Sandy's story."

"It's something else."

"Something we're keeping to ourselves?"

I got up and went to the fire. I have a theory about fires, that they like to be poked. I took the poker and moved one of the logs so that the configuration was different, enabling a small, suppressed flame to creep through to reach a new air pocket. The fire leaped, finding new life.

"A memory came back," I said as I sat down again. "I was at the Thanksgiving Day parade with my father."

"Is that what's upset you?"

"I have very few memories of my father. It was a shock when this one came back. I was vaguely aware that I'd seen the parade as a child, but I've never been able to see it in my mind. Or to see him."

He put his arm around me. "That's a nice memory," he said, "a father and his daughter at the parade. I remember going with my parents."

"It was while Sandy was telling me about his wife's disappearance that it came to me. It's as though there's a connection."

"There's no connection between anything he told you and your childhood. And you're under no obligation, moral or otherwise, to help him in a no-win case."

"I know."

"So tell me, what are you going to do?"

I smiled. He had gotten me completely off the hook but knew I would eventually do whatever I wanted. What I wanted was to have nothing to do with Natalie Gordon's disappearance. "I'm getting the dishes washed and then I'm going to read my book while you hit your books."

"Sounds like a great idea."

Hours later I had finished my book and he had put aside his law books. The fire had died a slow, natural death about an hour after we put the last log on, and the house was warm. Under the wonderful down comforter that I had bought with some of our wedding present money, we made love before going to sleep, our bodies warming the bed and each other, our love as sure and as satisfying as the day we pledged it.

Jack fell asleep soon after, but I was unable to. I try hard not to lie, but I often keep to myself things that I would rather not discuss. I had told him honestly about my unexpected recollection of being at the parade with my father, a recollection that was little more than a momentary snapshot. What I hadn't told him was that there was a third person in the picture, a woman, and it had not been my mother.

3

I met Melanie early Monday morning when I went out for my walk. It was really too cold to spend much time out of doors, and we did a quick circle of our block and parted. She didn't mention Sandy Gordon and I didn't either.

On Tuesday morning I taught my poetry course at a local college and then came home. It was the beginning of the spring semester and I was still getting to know my students, still trying to match names to faces. At home I had other work to do, preparing materials for Arnold Gold, my lawyer friend in New York who gave me away at my wedding last August. I was typing away at the ancient word processor he had given me when I thought I heard the doorbell ring. I saved my file, having long ago learned the consequences of not doing so, and went downstairs.

Sandy Gordon stood outside my front door, carrying a box big enough to hold a portable typewriter. "May I come in?"

"Sure." I felt a little disoriented, my head still on the legal brief I had been typing. "What brings you to Oakwood today?"

"You." He came in, put the box on the floor, and unbuttoned his coat. "Have you thought about it?"

"I have, yes."

He took his coat off and I hung it up, knowing this was an invitation for him to stay.

"You don't look very positive."

19

"Jack and I talked about it, Sandy. We both think that unless your wife caused her own disappearance, the chances of finding her alive are very small."

"I'm aware of that. I'm resigned to it, although no way do I believe she ran off."

"I thought about where I would start," I said, not responding to his forceful dissent to my suggestion, "who I would talk to, for example, and I came up blank. I can't believe there's anything on Seventy-fourth Street or anyone who was there that day that could help me."

"I agree with you. I think the parade isn't the place to start." He pointed at the carton on the floor. "I think that is. I've collected everything I could find in the house and put it all in that box. It's yours to look at, go through, whatever you want. Then make a decision."

"You're a very persuasive man. Does anyone ever say no to you?"

"All the time. But I don't want you to be one of them."

"Sandy, I feel very sad about your wife's disappearance."

"You're leading up to a no and I don't want to hear it. Will you do this for me? Go through the carton. OK?"

"I will."

"Thanks. We'll talk again."

Maybe that's why I do it, take on investigations that will lead me away from the safe and the ordinary, that innate desire to know about people's lives, where they've been, what they've done, what makes them tick, if anything. The carton sitting on the floor of my living room was too tempting to set aside. I lifted it onto the coffee table and pulled open the four flaps that had been neatly folded into each other. Since I was in my second year and fourth semester of teaching the same course, I had a great lesson plan prepared, and although I changed and updated it regularly, I had little to do to prepare for next Tuesday's class. And I would get to Arnold's work later. The carton won.

On top was a small, white leather photograph album that said OUR WEDDING in gold on the cover. The pages were plastic envelopes and each one was filled, front and back, with a picture the size of the page. The first few pages showed a bride dressing, a white, street-length dress going over her head, her carefully coiffed hair being brushed into place by a man with a brush and a very dedicated expression, mascara being applied in a mirror shot that focused on her reflection.

Sandy had not exaggerated. She was beautiful, with reddish brown hair and a smile as lovely as it was natural. The dress was simple and elegant, the short veil, when she finally had it put on, very fine-looking. There were a few snapshots also of the ceremony, which took place under the traditional canopy of a Jewish wedding. In one picture, Sandy was stamping on a white package on the floor, probably the glass he was to break to assure good luck to the couple. The luck hadn't lasted very long.

It was a small wedding, with the groom's father, gray-haired and considerably shorter than Sandy, a woman who was probably his sister, two children who were surely his. His bride, however, seemed to have only a single attendant, a pretty woman about her age in a peach-colored dress. If Natalie Gordon had had any other friends or any relatives, they had not attended, or at least not participated in the ceremony.

It struck me that my own wedding had resembled this one in some degree. My parents and aunt are gone, and except for my cousin Gene, I am pretty much without family. But I count all the nuns of St. Stephen's as my friends, and it was there that our wedding took place. Natalie had apparently come to Sandy without family.

None of the faces in the second half of the book looked familiar. I suppose second weddings are smaller and less lavish than first ones, and only the closest members of the circle are invited. The food looked wonderful, the guests at the handful of tables happy, and the final pictures of the couple being showered with rice a classic conclusion to a wedding.

I set the small album aside on the coffee table. I must admit I was itching to open my notebook and make some notes, not a good sign for someone who has turned down a case. I restrained myself and continued into the carton. There were a few books near the top—there seemed no organization to the contents; Sandy had probably just gathered things and stuffed them in—and I looked at them with interest. The first one was an anthology of modern American and English poetry, well read, from the look of the jacket. I opened it and found an inscription: "To Natalie with love forever, or for as long as it takes. Ron." The date was eight years ago. I leafed through the pages, but it was a thick book and I didn't notice anything special on the pages I saw.

The second book was quite different, a small, maroon leather-bound volume of *Othello*, the pages tipped with gold, surely part of a set and perhaps picked up in an antiquarian bookshop. This one had a surprising inscription: "To Scottie, For all the right reasons. With love, Natalie." Either it was a book she had given to Scottie and he had returned it, or she had inscribed it and never got to present it to him, or decided not to. In any case, it seemed a small treasure.

The last of the three books was another gift, a cookbook for a person living alone. The message in this one was, "To Natalie, So you don't cook your goose. Love, Mom." It was dated about seven years ago and was identified in no other way. At least Natalie had had one parent not too long ago.

There were envelopes of snapshots deeper in the carton. Sandy must have taken a camera with him everywhere they went, because there were pictures from the vacations he had described, pictures of their home, pictures taken both indoors and outdoors, with and without other people present, and even a few snapshots from the Thanksgiving Day parade. If I thought these last would give me a point of departure, I was disappointed. Most of them were of Macy's balloons, including Babar, coming down Central Park West far above where people stood watching them. There was only one picture of Natalie—proof, if I needed it, that she had gone to the parade—with her head raised in profile to look up at what was going by. There were no identifiable people, no balloon man, no hot dog man, no candy man.

The last envelope was quite different. It had a return address from a man with D.D.S. after his name. Inside were some copies of dental records and a letter, dated last year, written in layman's English to Sandy. It said that in discussions with Mrs. Gordon when she first visited him, she had acknowledged having orthodontia as an adult. From his own examination, he had been able to determine that Mrs. Gordon had had extensive cosmetic work done on her teeth, namely crowns on teeth he identified with numbers. Thus, I assumed, the perfect smile.

I set the letter and all the photographs aside with the books and looked at the rest of the things in the carton. For the most part they were quite impersonal. A copy of *New York* magazine was open to the middle of an article. A yellow telephone message said "Sandy" for the person called, "Marty" for the caller, and there were check marks next to TELEPHONED and PLEASE CALL. No message was written, but an *N* appeared at the bottom line. The piece of paper was undated and had no time on it.

An expensive-looking black satin evening bag with a gold frame and a long gold chain caught my eye and I took it out. Since I am now affluent enough to own two purses, I have discovered that I leave certain things in the one I'm not using, sometimes a receipt stuffed inside when I bought something or a memento of a place I have visited. This one was no different. Besides several carefully folded clean tissues, there was a folded card that said MR. AND MRS. SANDY GORDON on the outside and TABLE 12 on the inside. A matchbook from Lutèce indicated the kind of restaurants the Gordons frequented, and a small ivory comb attested to expensive taste. But there were no receipts, no notes, no scribblings.

A recipe file was filled mostly with recipes cut out of magazines and newspapers and occasionally some written for Natalie by other people. A few of them were on printed cards that said FROM THE RECIPE FILE OF, followed by a name. Although I went through the whole file, I found nothing written in Natalie's hand except a notation to bake a cake forty minutes instead of thirty-five.

There were a few other magazines in the carton, a post-card to Sandy and Natalie from Paris, two bottles of co-logne, two small bottles of perfume, all about half-full and all names that I recognized, a box of dusting powder, a toothbrush, a brush and comb, two lipsticks, one a pink shade, one on the orange side, both about half-used, several bottles of nail polish, and makeup including powder, rouge, moisturizer, base, mascara, and lotion to remove all of the above. Although these were certainly personal possessions, they didn't give me anything to go on, although I suppose I knew a little more about Natalie when I finished looking at them.

Down at the bottom, where it had probably dropped through the layers of disorganized items, was a key ring with several keys on it. None, I could see immediately, was for a safe-deposit box. One might have been for a suitcase, one or two for front doors, one small one just a mystery.

So that was Natalie Gordon's legacy. I assumed Sandy had her clothes in his home, perhaps other pocketbooks, too, but if he had hired a private detective, I had to believe all of that would have been expertly checked out. What was missing was a Social Security card, probably in the bag she had carried the day she disappeared, stubs from paychecks, tax returns for the last few years, at least for the few before she married, letters from family or friends, diaries, almost anything in her handwriting. Some of those things, credit cards, a pocket agenda, a shopping list, might have been in the bag she was carrying. But records of past jobs would have been filed away somewhere. I learned when I married Jack that he keeps all of his records in case the IRS has questions years hence. Following his example, I began to do the same.

But Natalie Gordon hadn't, or Sandy hadn't thought such records were relevant. He had said that this carton was the place to start, but having looked through it, I still didn't know where to go from here. No cosmetics counter was likely to give me a lead, nor was Lutèce, where she had enjoyed a meal. Her choice of magazines told me something about her, as did the books, but unless I could identify the men who had given and received them, they were pretty useless.

I had opened the carton with an almost breathless anticipation. Now I felt disappointed. Knowing what Natalie looked like, sniffing her perfume and looking at the shade of pink she chose for her cheeks, touching the evening bag she carried to Lutèce, were all very interesting but gave me no clue as to what had happened to her. Nor did they give me any clue as to who she was or what her life had been like before Sandy Gordon married her.

I put everything back, more or less in the order in which I had taken it out, leaving the keys for last. But they, too, needed a name or address to be hung on. Whatever doors they opened were as firmly locked as the doors to Natalie Gordon's past.

I went back upstairs to finish my work for Arnold.

4

I drove into the city with Jack the next morning. Before he reached the Sixty-fifth Precinct in Brooklyn, he dropped me at a subway station and I went into Manhattan to Arnold Gold's office. When I was finished there, I would take the train back to Oakwood and Jack would go to his classes. As I put my coat on before I left the house, I saw the carton. I had talked to Jack about it very briefly when he came home the night before, exhausted as usual. I could tell he didn't like the idea of Sandy dropping in uninvited, and he had no desire to look at anything in the box.

In the last few days my own memories of the Thanksgiving Day parade had started to come back with greater clarity. I now recalled that my father had taken me to see it several times, and he had looked forward to those annual morning trips with an eagerness as great as my own. But there was something odd about those trips, something that didn't quite make sense. On the drive into the city, I asked Jack about it.

"On the morning of the Thanksgiving Day parade, my father used to drive us in and then we took the subway the rest of the way. I don't know what stop we got off at, but I remember we used to see the Statue of Liberty."

"In the harbor?"

"That's what's so weird. It was near the parade. We walked down a street and saw it."

"Sixty-fourth," he said without hesitating. "Between

26

Broadway and Central Park West, north side of the street."

"So it wasn't a crazy dream."

"There's some company in that building, or there used to be. Liberty something. She's on the roof."

"Then that must be where we watched the parade from, Sixty-fourth and Central Park West."

"There's a big building there, Ethical Culture, I think. Takes up the block between Sixty-fourth and Sixty-third."

"It seemed like such a crazy memory, the parade and the Statue of Liberty."

"You don't talk about your father much."

"I don't remember much about him. This memory really came out of the blue."

"Here OK?" He was slowing the car, my subway station just across the street.

"Fine." I leaned over and we kissed. "See you tonight."

He grinned at me and touched my shoulder as I opened the car door. On the sidewalk I waved and he took off.

"So we got you instead of a FedEx package." Arnold Gold was standing at his secretary's desk as I came in.

"You said you had some more work," I said. "Good morning. Nice to see you all."

The phone rang on the secretary's desk and Arnold said, "Let's get to work, friends."

He took me out to lunch, one of the fringe benefits of working in his office. Arnold is not a one-restaurant man. There are days he wants a salad, other days a delicatessen sandwich, or a big bowl of soup and nothing else. Today he thought we'd try a new pasta restaurant that had opened about a month earlier, and he had noticed that the crowd had diminished, although his gourmet colleagues had assured him it was worth the walk. We walked, fighting the winds of downtown Manhattan. When we arrived, my face was so stiff with cold, I could hardly talk. But his colleagues were right.

"Looks like a good menu," Arnold said, putting his glasses on to read it. "I think I'll try this one with the clams and red sauce."

"I'm going for the primavera."

"Because you want spring to come. Will it be enough to keep you happy all afternoon?"

"You know what I usually have for lunch, Arnold."

"I noticed the tuna fish market collapsed after you got married. You must make better lunches for Jack than you used to eat yourself."

"I do. But I haven't given up tuna fish altogether."

A wonderful machine was spinning out miles of fresh pasta and I watched it for a minute.

"Looks like we get a free show."

"It's a very pretty place."

"So how've you been since Christmas? We still haven't stopped talking about St. Stephen's. What a beautiful place that is. What a remarkable woman your friend Sister Joseph is."

"Yes on both counts. We've been fine. Something just came up the other day."

"Uh-oh."

I laughed. "You smell it, don't you?"

"Find a body under your bed?"

"Melanie's uncle's wife—young, beautiful, second marriage—"

"Usual story."

"Right. She disappeared during the Thanksgiving Day parade the year before last."

"And he wants you to find her. I wouldn't touch it."

"Why not?"

"She probably ran off with the milkman and doesn't want to come back. They still deliver milk out where you live?"

"A couple of times a week."

"I can remember the clip-clop of the horses' hooves at six in the morning. And that was every day."

"You're just trying to impress me with how old you are."

"Just with how good my memory is."

"There's something else, Arnold."

Our lunches arrived at that moment and we were both impressed at how beautiful they looked. I am not only a very ordinary cook, I am the least artistic one I've ever met. My attempts at arranging food to look like the dishes I see on television have been thoroughly without success. But here was a deep dish of swirling pasta interlaced with colorful vegetables and a fragrant sauce that made my mouth water.

"Well, I knew lawyers were good for something," Arnold said, digging in. "They always know the best new restaurants."

"So do cops."

"Cops are always thinking of their stomachs."

I laughed, but it was true. "Is that prejudice?"

"Pure truth based on years of observation. You were saying there was something else." Arnold never forgets where he is in a conversation, what the last witness mumbled in his testimony, what a member of the group said under his breath that he wishes everyone would forget.

"Talking to this man about his missing wife, I remembered something about my own childhood. My father used to take me to the parade."

He looked at me, waiting for me to continue.

"I think I know where we watched it from because I remember seeing a small Statue of Liberty on top of a building."

"There is one up there, you're right."

"Jack says it's on Sixty-fourth."

"I'm sure he knows his geography a lot better than I know mine."

"My father met a woman there while we watched the parade."

"I run into people I know all the time in New York, Chrissie. Harriet sees people in stores and on the streets; I see them in courtrooms and restaurants, and if I went to parades, I'd probably see them there, too."

"It wasn't like that. And it wasn't just once. They met there. They were looking for each other."

"And it's thrown you into a tizzy."

"I'm afraid it has."

"Did he have a sister?"

"Yes, my aunt Meg. That's the only one."

"And you want to find a woman you met a couple of times fifteen or twenty years ago?"

"More like twenty-five."

"Sounds like you've got your work cut out for you."

"I've started to wonder—"

"Don't wonder, Chrissie," he said firmly. "Your mother told you he died. He died. Your mother was an honorable woman."

"She spent her whole life protecting me."

He reached over and patted my hand. "And you met me in spite of it and you married a good cop."

I smiled and nodded, feeling teary. Arnold is the father who replaced my natural father. I met him while I was investigating a forty-year-old murder shortly after I left St. Stephen's. He gave me work so that I could join his medical plan, and I've stayed with the work since my marriage because I love it and I love him. I enjoy the trip into the city, the occasional visits to one court or another in downtown Manhattan, the opportunity to be part of a world different from the one I live and teach in.

"I want to try, Arnold," I said. "Just see if I can find something."

"And this other thing, the woman who disappeared, she's your excuse."

"Sort of." I twisted some pasta on my fork and speared a nice piece of red pepper. How hard could it be to make something like this? I wondered, enjoying the tastes. Probably harder than boiling spaghetti. "It's intriguing, Arnold, a woman turning a corner and never seen again. He said when he finally went to look for her, a couple of minutes later, he saw a single balloon floating up to the sky."

"Very romantic, doesn't mean a thing. Some kid who wouldn't hang on tight let go a balloon and suddenly we have high drama."

"You're incorrigible, Arnold."

"Join the crowd. It's how I'm listed in the directory of the ABA."

"This is a great lunch."

"And you're great company. I expect you want to take a little ride up the west side to Sixty-fourth Street as long as you're in the city."

"I have work to do."

"It can wait till tomorrow."

"So can Sixty-fourth Street."

"Just keep me posted. These are two hopeless efforts. I give you a fifty-fifty shot at finding some answers."

"As usual, I think you overrate my abilities."

I was able to finish the work for Arnold before three and I took the Broadway subway up to Sixty-sixth Street, the Lincoln Center area. I came up to street level on a triangular island with traffic going off in more directions than I could count. I was at the point where Broadway veered east on its southerly route, crossing Columbus Avenue, which ran parallel to it for miles uptown. Broadway is a strange street, going from northwest Manhattan to the southeast, intersecting with one avenue after another so that eventually it runs east of Fifth Avenue when it starts out west of Eighth Avenue. All these intersections leave chaos in their

wake, triangles, rerouted traffic, complicated lights, and ir-
rational traffic patterns.

I made my way down to Sixty-fourth and looked at the
rooftops of the old, five-story buildings that still lined part
of the street. There she was, a green Statue of Liberty a
couple of stories high poised on a roof. My heart was beat-
ing as though I'd made a discovery when all I'd done was
reach a place on a street. I walked along the south side of
Sixty-fourth toward Central Park West, passing Liberty
Storage, the building on the north side that sported the
statue. The block was mostly residential, partly high-rise,
partly smaller old buildings. As Jack had remembered, the
Ethical Culture Society occupied the corner and stretched
south along Central Park West.

I crossed Sixty-fourth and turned north. The number of
people who lived on Sixty-fourth and the block of Central
Park West from there to Sixty-fifth had to be enormous,
had to be in the thousands. But I was sure the street was
significant. If we got off the subway at Sixty-sixth, the
most natural thing to do would have been to walk directly
east to Central Park West. But we hadn't. The woman must
have had a connection to Sixty-fourth Street.

Across Central Park West was the western edge of Central Park, a green anomaly in the center of concrete Manhattan. I kept walking north. At Sixty-sixth a road pierced
the park, and through the trees I could see the Tavern on
the Green. I speeded up my pace and continued north.

Seventy-fourth Street, where Natalie Gordon had disappeared, was as bland and unavailing of secrets as every
other corner I had passed on my way. There was nothing
exceptional, nothing different, nothing even interesting,
about the corner. I looked at the facade of the large, magnificent building facing the park. A doorman in uniform
came out with a well-dressed woman and hailed a taxi for
her. She was wearing fur and high heels and she sat inside
the cab for only a second before it pulled from the curb.

Otherwise, there was nothing, a few walkers, not surprising on a day as cold as this, a small amount of traffic, a single dog with its well-trained master ready to scoop at first need.

I turned down Seventy-fourth and walked the block to Columbus Avenue. Up here, Broadway was two blocks and one triangle west of Central Park West. The street was lined with town houses with plenty of doorways that a woman could be dragged into. I looked at each of them as I passed. At Columbus I continued on to Amsterdam, then turned left to find the subway at Seventy-second where Broadway and Amsterdam converged. I got an express, made a change at Times Square, and shuttled over to Grand Central Station. I caught the last train home before the rush hour.

I told Jack about my father and the woman when he got home.

"That's what's been bothering you," he said. We were sitting at the kitchen table, he eating some warmed-up stew left over from a meal I had cooked over the weekend.

"I want to find out more about it."

"Why?"

"Curiosity."

"What are you afraid of? That your father had a girl-friend?"

"I don't know. I don't really believe he did, but I'm sure she was someone he knew, someone he met by appointment, not accident, at least after the first time."

"You think you met her more than once?"

"I'm sure of it. I'm sure I went to the parade more than once and I'm sure she was there each time."

"What about this Sandy Gordon thing?"

"I'll give it a try. But only if he has more to tell me. With what I have now in that carton, I don't have enough to go on. He must be holding something else, some papers or something. She must have filed a tax return that would tell me where she worked. If not, that's it."

"Where are you starting on your father's case?"

I had thought about that. "I guess downtown Manhattan where he worked—if the company is still there."

"You know where to turn if you need help."

"Thanks." I leaned over and kissed him. "Anyone ever tell you you're a peach?"

"Yeah, but I kissed her good-bye years ago."

5

"Is my uncle driving you crazy?"

Mel and I were taking our morning constitutional together. It's how we met just after I moved into the house I inherited from my aunt. While we do it less in the cold weather, we both found ourselves out on this crisp winter morning.

"Not crazy. I think his problem is driving him crazy, though."

"He asked you to help?"

"At your brunch on Sunday. Then he dropped over on Tuesday afternoon and gave me a carton of stuff about his wife."

"Do you mind?"

"Of course not, Mel. He's living in limbo, not knowing what's become of her."

"I think she ran away because something in her past caught up with her."

"You sound like you've thought about it. What makes you feel that's what happened?"

"What else could it be? Sandy's rich, adoring, the kind of husband women would die for. They weren't even married a year. I don't know if he's told you, but they found out a few very strange things about her after she disappeared."

"Like what?"

"Like she was born yesterday. Like she came into exis-

35

tence when she was about thirty years old. No history before that. Sounds like a secret life, don't you think?"

"Possibly," I said cautiously.

"I don't know how you can marry a person you don't know anything about."

"What did Jack know about me?"

"Enough. You were Mrs. Wirth's niece, you'd spent fifteen years at St. Stephen's with a lot of respectable people to vouch for you. I would have provided a reference, if needed." Melanie is a fierce friend. "And you weren't Natalie."

"What does that mean?"

"I never met her, Chris. What I know is family gossip. But he picked her up—"

"Where?"

"At one of the more acceptable places to pick people up, a museum or lecture. And they started dating. She claimed to have no family, not a lot of friends, and an autobiography that turned out to be full of holes."

"How did you know Sandy talked to me about her?"

"He called last night. He must have tried you and you weren't home. He'll probably call again today."

"I'll be in and out," I said. "But I think if we're going to work together, I should have his number so I can call him."

"Are you working together?"

"Maybe," I said. "I'm intrigued."

"I'll give you his number when I get home."

I left Sandy's number near the kitchen phone and took care of some errands I had to run, thinking about the woman whose past might have caught up with her. It was hard for me to imagine what those words meant. There was very little about my own life that was mysterious or that I kept secret. I had been eight, almost nine, when my father died My mother had been widowed over five years when she herself succumbed. During those years I went from child to teenager, from grade school to high school. She gave me a wonderful life that included home-baked cookies, family, enough new clothes that I never felt I needed anything, and she worked until her illness prevented her from leaving the house. She never let me forget I had had a good father, but she never let me feel my life was lacking because he was no longer around. Everyone seems to be looking for role models nowadays. I don't have far to look. Anything I needed was available in my family.

But maybe Natalie Gordon hadn't been so lucky. Perhaps even finding a husband as wonderful as the one Mel had described hadn't been enough to protect her from old ghosts, whatever they might be.

When I got back to the house, I called Sandy Gordon.

"What did you think of the stuff in the box?" he asked.

"Before we get into that, we need to agree on some ground rules."

"Does that mean you're taking the case?"

"It means I'm considering it. Mel gave me your phone number this morning. We have to work together, Sandy. You can't drop in on me without calling first, and I have to be able to call you when I need to."

"No problem there. I apologize for coming unannounced. I had called Tuesday morning and you weren't home. I didn't feel like leaving a message."

"You told me the carton had information that would give me a point of departure. I didn't find any. What I found is what Natalie looked like, her cosmetics and perfume, her incomplete dental record, and not much else. I need a lot more. She must have worked at some time, and I want to know for whom, where, what she earned, the kind of work she did. I want to know who her maid of honor was at the wedding and other personal acquaintances she had. I'd like to know where she was living when you met her and any previous addresses that you know of."

"Whoa! Hold on. You're going too fast. I'm trying to write all this down. There's no problem getting you anything you've mentioned so far. I've got IRS returns from the year we were married—I didn't have that when I hired the detective, by the way. I've got her maid of honor's address and phone number, and the address she was living at when I met her. Go on."

"Do you know anything about the keys?"

"What keys?"

"The ring of keys in the box."

"I don't what you're talking about. I don't remember any ring of keys."

"They were in the bottom of the box."

"I assumed her house keys were in the purse she was carrying on Thanksgiving Day."

"Then these must have fallen out of something you gave me."

"Interesting."

I must admit it gave me a prickle of excitement. "We'll look at them together when I see you."

"How soon?"

I looked at my watch. "It's too late for me to drive down to New Jersey today."

"You don't have to make the trip unless you want to see the house for some reason. Let me get these papers together and bring them to you. What's convenient?"

"Tomorrow," I said without hesitating. I always like to start a new project on a new day. "I'm an early riser."

"I'll be there between nine and nine-thirty."

"You knew I'd do it, didn't you?" I asked Jack when we were getting ready for bed that evening. His law school is four nights a week, and there's a sense of relief when he gets home Thursday night.

"I think you want to do it because you hold out hope that there's a chance she's still alive."

"I do. Not much, but I don't think it's hopeless."

"I can probably get a look at the file if you want me to."

"Sure. I doubt there's anything there that'll help me, but I should look. Sandy says he has some papers at home that he didn't have when she disappeared, her tax returns for that year."

"That's a start."

"And the name of her maid of honor. She may have been Natalie's only friend in the New York area."

"Was Natalie from out of town?"

"I don't know. I don't know if he knows."

"Sounds like a funny marriage."

"That's what Mel says. But so what? She's somebody and she's missing."

"Can I ask you the other question?"

I drew a blank. "What question?"

"About your father. You going to pursue that, too?"

"I'm going to try."

"Well, these may be the shortest investigations you've done so far."

For a smart guy, he can be amazingly wrong sometimes.

Jack backed out of the driveway the next morning seconds before Sandy Gordon drove up it. He came inside with an attaché case, and while I put some coffee on, he opened it and spread papers out on the dining room table. The table is old, somewhat scarred, and due to be replaced, which is why I invited him to use it. I like to spread out there myself when I have a lot of papers to look at and don't know which one I'll need next.

"Here's our marriage certificate from the State of New Jersey," he said when I joined him. "And the Jewish one."

"How beautiful," I said in surprise. "I've never seen one before." It was colorful and printed in Hebrew. Two signatures appeared on blank lines, his and hers, and some other names were lettered in. "Who are these people?"

"Our witnesses. They're both friends of mine, so I don't think talking to them will get you anything."

"When we were married we were asked if we'd been married before and to produce proof of divorce if we were."

"She said she wasn't. I was and I had my divorce papers with me."

"Her maiden name was Miller."

"Right."

"Do you know where she was from?"

"Not specifically."

I waited for him to elaborate. Both Mel and Jack had found it hard to believe a man could marry someone about whom he knew so little. While I felt I wouldn't have been able to do it myself, the pictures of Natalie offered an explanation. Sandy had been infatuated with the beautiful younger woman he had met after his marriage broke up. What he did might not have been altogether rational, but it was understandable.

"I got a lot of flak from my family," he said. "They wanted to know who her family was, what her background was. What she told me satisfied me. I loved her, Chris. She loved me. We had a great marriage."

"What did she tell you?" I took my notebook and opened it to a fresh page.

"Her parents died when she was young. She was an only child and was raised by relatives she didn't specially care for and they moved around a lot. When she graduated high school, she packed a bag and came to New York."

It was a story that would fly or fail depending on the skepticism and gullibility of the listener. Surely it was true for a large number of Americans. As a teacher in both Catholic and secular schools, I have heard a good sample of improbable stories from students. Some of them have actually been true.

"Did she ever talk about inviting any family to the wedding?"

"No."

"Where did she say she came from?"

"She said there were a lot of places, mostly in Indiana. She didn't like to talk about it because they weren't happy years. By the way, I'm no expert, but she didn't talk like a native New Yorker."

That was a useful observation. I'm not an expert either, but like most people, I can pick out a southern accent, a midwestern one, a New England one. "Where did she work, Sandy?"

He took a piece of paper from a leather holder in his pocket and wrote. "It's a fairly new advertising company, one of those places where a couple of young hotshots got together and started making money. They've expanded a lot since they opened their shop, but she was with them for a couple of years."

"Why did she leave?"

"Essentially because we were getting married. I didn't want her making the trip into New York every day, and she didn't want to either. We bought a house when we got married and I wanted her to make it hers, fix it up her way. She decided to make it a full-time job, at least at the beginning."

I looked at the name and address, Hopkins and Jewell. The address was downtown Manhattan, near Union Square. "Where did she work before this?"

"I don't know."

"She never mentioned a previous job?"

"Not that I remember. And I didn't find any old tax returns anywhere."

"Strange. My husband keeps his for years."

"So do I. Maybe she worked for Hopkins longer than I thought. You know what? Let me call my accountant. I bet he can get hold of her old returns from the IRS. May I use your phone?"

"Sure. It's in the kitchen."

It wasn't a long conversation. Sandy was on first names with his accountant, a man he called Alfie. I could tell as soon as the small talk was over that Sandy was being given a hard time. He hung up shaking his head. "Can't get them," he said to me.

I brought the coffee into the dining room and poured for both of us. He took milk and no sugar; I always drink mine black. "Seems strange," I said. "You're her husband."

"Doesn't matter. Apparently the IRS is very strict about giving out information. For me to get her returns, or vice versa, I'd need a power of attorney from her. He gave me the form number, as though it mattered. If she were here to sign it, I wouldn't need the damn thing."

"So the government keeps the past a secret," I said. "I'm not exactly sorry to hear that, except it makes my job harder."

"I suppose we could try for a court order."

"I'm not in a position to get one and I'm not sure a court will give one even to you. Your wife apparently walked out on you. There's no evidence of foul play, there was no ransom demand. Why should a judge let you in on secrets she kept from you when you were living together?"

"I thought you were on my side."

"I am," I said. "I'm just—"

"I know, I know. It's the kind of runaround I've been getting for over a year."

"Tell me about her maid of honor."

"Susan Diggins. Nice woman. Just got married a couple of months ago. I've got her new name written down. She and Natalie met at Hopkins and Jewell and became friends. Susan left there before Natalie did, got a better job, I think."

"Did they ever live together?"

"I don't know. I'm not sure. They may have. You'll have to ask her." He took an envelope out of his jacket pocket and put it on the table. "I've got Susan's name and address in here and the last address Natalie lived at before we married."

"Good." I took the key ring out of my pants pocket where I'd tucked it this morning and laid it on the table. "Do they look familiar?"

He picked the keys up and held them on his palm. "This one could be a house key, but it doesn't look like the key to our house." He reached into his own pocket and took out a large ring of keys. "This one's the key to our house."

There was no similarity. "Maybe they're from an old apartment," I suggested.

"No car keys here. This one looks like a key to a suitcase. I bought Natalie luggage before we were married. I think it used a combination lock of some kind."

"Did you pack the carton you gave me?"

"Not exactly. She kept some pictures in there, in big envelopes, and I just added the other things. Those keys could have been there all along and I wouldn't have known it."

"Did the detective you hired look through the pictures?"

"He really wasn't too interested. He wanted one good full-face picture and I gave it to him."

"OK," I said. "Now, if you wouldn't mind, I want to hear the story of how you met, how you fell in love, everything you can think of."

"I'll need some more coffee," he said, looking uneasy.

6

"After my divorce, I moved into an apartment. At first it was a relief just to live in peace and quiet. I saw my kids every weekend and I went to work, and sometimes I took in a movie or visited friends. After a couple of months I got restless. I'd drop into bars, go to parties, let myself be fixed up by well-meaning friends. Some of the women I met were nice and I enjoyed going out with them, but in the end, I think they all wanted to get married, sooner rather than later, and I didn't know if I wanted to.

"But I wanted their company. I like women. They add to your life. Once, when the pickings got a little lean, I even advertised in *New York* magazine. I got seventy-six answers in a week, one of them from my ex-wife."

"Oh my," I said.

"I never let her know. It's all done anonymously till you write to an advertiser. It was interesting to see how she described herself, even more interesting to see the picture she used. She'd gotten herself all made up and had one of those glamour shots taken. If I'd been someone else, I probably would have called her.

"Anyway, if I didn't have a date on Saturday night, I'd go into the city and try to pick up a single ticket for a play or a concert. I like that sort of thing and sometimes you meet people at intermission. One Sunday afternoon I took myself over to the Metropolitan Museum of Art. I hadn't been to the Egyptian section for a long time and they had some new stuff I wanted to see. I went into that big room that's all glass and light, and there she was."

"Natalie," I said.

"Natalie. She was just standing and looking at the temple as though she was totally lost in it. She was wearing a big rose-colored sweater, black leather pants, and she had her coat over one arm. I went over, not too close, and looked at it myself. It was a winter day, not very sunny, and all the light in the room seemed to focus on her."

There's not much you can do when a man is hooked. I let Sandy go on for a while, describing this and that about Natalie, how they exchanged their first words, how they sort of but not quite walked together to another chamber, how they went out of the museum in each other's company and went to one place for a drink and another place for dinner.

Was Natalie waiting in the museum that winter afternoon to be picked up? Who knows? Did I ever visit a museum on a weekend afternoon when I was single? Yes, I certainly did. Did I do it to meet men? Most assuredly not. And in the end, what difference did it make?

The tale went on, the immediate "chemistry" between the two of them, the frequent dates, the movement toward intimacy.

"Was she always available when you called?" I asked.

"As a matter of fact, no." He seemed a little surprised at the question.

"Did you think it was because she was going out with other men or because she wanted you to think she was?"

"What does that have to do with anything?"

"Sandy, you said you would answer my questions. We're talking about a real person, someone who is old enough to have had experience with men, to know how to handle them. I'm wondering if there's someone she left when she met you."

"Someone she might have gone back to," he said wryly.

That was exactly what I was thinking. "Someone who might know something about her," I said gently.

"I can't tell you that."

"Did you visit her at her apartment?"

"I usually picked her up there."

"Were there signs of anyone else around? Cigarettes? Clothes that didn't look like hers?"

"Nothing."

"Did she cook for you?"

"Infrequently."

"Where did you go to eat?"

"Restaurants, mostly in Manhattan."

"Did you ever meet any of her friends?"

"Never. We sometimes went out with friends of mine."

"I'm going to start with Susan Diggins," I said, "and go on from there. Maybe one day I'll come out and see the house, but at the moment, unless you've got cartons of stuff stashed away, I can't see any reason to. I assume your detective talked to Susan, too."

"I'm sure he did."

"And to Hopkins and Jewell."

"He went down there." He picked the keys up off the table and looked at them. "I wish I knew where these came from," he said.

"Sandy, if you find any old pocketbooks of Natalie's, would you look inside them and see if there's anything that could give me a lead? And don't throw anything away, even little scraps."

"I'll take care of it."

"Did she have any charge accounts before you married?"

"I don't think so. I filled out a lot of forms for her so she could open them. They were essentially in my name because I had the income. I got the feeling she'd always used cash."

"Did any bills come in after she disappeared?"

"Yes, but they were department store bills, the clothes I

told you she bought for our winter vacation. Nothing was dated after Thanksgiving Day."

"And I assume she wrote no checks and took no money out of the bank after that date."

"Nothing." He said it with a sense of satisfaction. He was proving to me that he was right, that she had not left of her own free will.

"I'll keep you posted," I said, closing our conversation.

He took a wallet out of his pocket and counted out some bills. Then he laid five hundred-dollar bills on the table. I stared at them. The first time I ever saw a bill that large was in the supermarket in Oakwood after I moved here. "I don't need it," I said.

"Then put it away and use it when you do. Mel says you're honest. I trust you."

"I'll account for every cent."

He gave me a smile. "Every dollar'll do. Just come up with something."

The address and phone number of Susan Diggins Hartswell were in the envelope as promised. She lived in a Westchester suburb that I could drive to in less than an hour. Although I assumed she was still working and wouldn't answer her home phone, I dialed the number and was rewarded by having her pick up.

"Mrs. Hartswell," I said, "my name is Christine Bennett and I'm a friend of Sandy Gordon." I used the word loosely and to good effect.

"Yes. Has something happened? Has Natalie turned up?"

"I'm afraid not. Sandy has asked me to look into her disappearance."

"It's been so long now," she said sadly. "I don't know what you can do at this point. I talked to the detective he hired last year and that didn't lead anywhere."

"I have a little experience investigating and maybe I'll

turn up something the detective missed. I'd like to start by talking to you."

"Well, I'm home being pregnant, so I'm available and I want to do everything I can to help. So name your time."

"This afternoon if you're free."

"Let's see. If you can be here by twelve-thirty, we can talk over lunch. I cook salt-free, but I'll let you add salt at the table."

"That's fine. I'll see you then."

I had a chicken ready to pop into the oven (recipe courtesy of Melanie Gross) when I got home, so I felt pretty free as I got into my car and started to drive.

I would be lying if I didn't admit that starting an investigation gives me a high. This one was different from all the others in several ways. I had never known Natalie and didn't really know Sandy. I hadn't stumbled on a body, and in a sense I had no personal interest in the subject of the investigation, although I was developing one simply because I'm me.

What concerned me most was that I was following in the footsteps of a professional and that unless someone said something new or Sandy turned up some fresh piece of evidence, I would go no further than the detective had. What I had working for me was that people sometimes open up more readily to a woman, someone not in a uniform, someone not professional. Also, I enjoy what I do. It makes a difference.

The Hartswells lived on a pleasant suburban street lined with houses that had once probably resembled each other more than they did today. They had been built along a couple of general designs and changed through creative landscaping, additions, some second stories added on ranches, and a variety of windows. I parked at the curb in front of a two-story white house with bright blue trim, and went up a concrete walk to the front door.

Susan Hartswell was well into her pregnancy. She opened the door and we introduced ourselves as she took my coat.

"Has anything new come up?" she asked as I followed her to the kitchen.

"Nothing that I know of. Sandy is desperate to find her."

"Sit where you feel comfortable. They're both the same." She was referring to two attractive fruit salads.

"Where'd you find such beautiful fruit at this time of year?" I asked.

"We have a great produce market in the next town. They fly stuff in from South America and California, and most of it is pretty good. You can drink juice or bottled water. I cleaned out all the tea and coffee when I got pregnant so I wouldn't be tempted."

I accepted juice and we dug in. "I have no record of what the detective asked you, or the police, so if I sound repetitive, please bear with me. Do you know how old Natalie is?"

"Probably older than she told Sandy. I'm thirty-six and she said she was three years younger than me, but I'd guess she's my age, give or take a year."

"What makes you think so?"

"Little things she dropped about high school graduation and what she was doing when Kennedy got shot."

That was good thinking. I was talking to someone who used her head. "Do you remember when she met Sandy?"

"Maybe three years ago. Then they got married about two years ago. They weren't married for long."

"Do you remember where she met him?"

"In one of the museums, I think. I didn't go with her that day."

"Did you go together sometimes?"

"Lots of times."

"To pick up men?"

"To see the exhibits and meet interesting people. You can meet men that way. Not a lot, but it happens."

"How long have you known her?"

"I probably met her about four years ago. Maybe four and a half."

"Where?"

"At this advertising agency we worked for. Hopkins and Jewell. She was there when they hired me."

"And you just became friends."

"We went to dinner sometimes, saw a play, gossiped about office things."

"Did you meet any of her other friends?"

"Not that I remember. I don't think she'd been in New York very long."

"Where had she come from?"

"Somewhere in the Midwest. She sounded Midwest."

I ate a juicy piece of watermelon. "Had she been married before?"

Susan didn't answer right away. For the first time she seemed to weigh her words. "Natalie wasn't the kind of person to let it all hang out. You always got the feeling about her that there was a lot beneath the surface. I respected her for it. She never told me she'd been married before. In fact, she told me she hadn't been. But I thought there might have been someone once who meant a lot to her, someone she'd had a hard time forgetting. It doesn't mean she was married."

"But you got the feeling she wanted to settle down."

"We both did. She wanted to get married, to have a baby, to be a family person, but she wanted to do it with the right man. She wanted to love him."

"Did she love Sandy?"

"Passionately."

"I saw your picture in the Gordons' wedding album. You were Natalie's maid of honor. Tell me about the wedding."

"It was small, tasteful, expensive, traditional."

"How did she do with Sandy's relatives?"

"There were only a handful of relatives there. I'd guess most of the guests were his old friends and their wives. He joked that one of the men had gone to kindergarten with him."

"She get along with them?"

"Natalie gets along with people. She knows how. Wherever she is now, she's getting along."

We had finished our salads and Susan moved the plates to the kitchen counter. "Feel like a cookie?" she asked.

"No thanks."

She smiled. "Bless you. If you'd had one, I'd have had to join you, and I don't need the calories. I just keep them in the house because of my husband."

"You're really doing everything right, aren't you?"

"You have to. In the dark ages—when I was born—there was so much people didn't know. They ate the wrong foods and drank the wrong drinks, they were afraid to exercise. This may be my only child, and I'm doing it right because with a baby, you can't go back and correct your mistakes."

I kept my opinion of her rather strong views on child-bearing and generation gaps to myself, but I was pleased she had led into a subject that I wanted to ask about. "Did Natalie confide to you that she was pregnant before she disappeared?"

It was the second time she paused and considered. "She didn't know for sure, but she thought she might be. She was waiting to be tested. She was supposed to go the Monday after Thanksgiving."

"I see."

"Sandy had changed his mind about having a baby. When they were dating, he said he didn't want another child. He has a couple of older children from his first marriage and he didn't want to start over at his age."

"But she married him anyway, even though she wanted a baby."

"I told you, she was crazy about him."

"Had she told Sandy her suspicion?"

"No. She wanted to surprise him when she knew for sure."

"It's nice that he changed his mind," I said. "It really shows the marriage was working."

"It was working. It was a great marriage. And I'll tell you something. I was jealous to the core when she said she might be pregnant. I can't tell you how much I wanted a baby. Do you have kids?"

"I was just married last summer."

"Don't wait too long. The clock is ticking."

"What clock?"

"Your biological clock. Let that body of yours do what it was born to do."

I promised her I would. "You've been very helpful, Sue, and it's been a great lunch."

"Anything," she said with feeling. "I want her found. I want to know what happened to her."

"I'll do my best. Do you happen to know where she lived before this address?" I showed her the one Sandy had given me.

She shook her head. "That's where she lived when I met her. I think she said she'd moved there around the time she started working at Hopkins."

"Do you know if she ever had a roommate?"

"No idea. She didn't when I met her."

"Old boyfriends?" I asked.

"She went out, but if there was anyone important, I don't think I knew about him. She would mention names sometimes, but mostly first names. I'm sorry I can't help you."

"You've helped me a lot." I opened my bag and took out the ring of keys. "Do you recognize these?"

She shook her head. "Can't say I do, can't say I don't. Should I?"

"I don't know." I wrote my name, address, and phone

number on a piece of paper and gave it to her. "In case you think of anything. Did you tell the detective substantially what you told me?"

"Substantially. I didn't tell him she thought she was pregnant."

"Why not?"

"He didn't ask and I didn't think it was his business."

"Thank you for telling me."

"Thank you for talking about her in the present tense."

I had noticed she had done the same. I shook her hand, wished her well, and got my coat. Outside it was still bitter cold. As I walked to the car, for the first time I thought I heard my biological clock ticking.

7

It was two o'clock when I started the car and ten after when I spotted a pay phone. I didn't know if Friday afternoon was a good time to call for an appointment, but I wanted to get one at Hopkins and Jewell as soon as possible. A very self-possessed sounding woman answered and I told her I was looking into the disappearance of Natalie Miller Gordon and wanted to talk to someone who had known her.

"Is this concerned with her disappearance?"

"Yes, it is."

"Who do you represent?"

I told her I was working for Sandy Gordon.

"I'll have to check it out, ma'am, before I can make an appointment."

I told her that would be fine and she put me on hold. I took some more quarters out of my bag and waited. I always carry quarters with me because they're good for parking meters as well as pay phones. I haven't yet come to terms with credit cards, although if I ever do, it's my shoulder that will benefit.

"He says it's OK," she said, coming back sooner than I expected. "When would you like to come in?"

"I can probably be there in an hour."

"I'll squeeze you in when you get here."

* * *

I had surprised myself by saying I would drive into the city, but where I was calling from was closer to New York than where I lived, so it made sense to go from here instead of waiting for Monday and going from Oakwood. Besides, the sooner is always the better.

There was little traffic until I got below Forty-second Street, and it picked up again when I got on Eighteenth Street and drove east. When I was more or less in the area of Hopkins and Jewell, I started looking around for a meter. I realized pretty quickly this was silly on two counts. One was, there weren't any free, and the other was that Sandy had given me money for just this purpose. But I admit to having pangs of conscience when I drove into a parking garage.

An attractive young woman sat inside the door of the office and gave me a radiant smile. My name rang a bell and she made a call after asking me to take a seat.

"I have Christine Bennett here," I heard her say. Then, "We'll be right there." She stood and invited me to join her. She was wearing a very short suede skirt and a matching vest over a black blouse. At a door at the end of the hall, she knocked, waited, then opened it. "Go right in," she said.

To my surprise, the person who rose from behind the desk was a handsome woman in her thirties, dressed to kill in a pin-striped suit with a silk blouse showing at the neck, fingernails longer than mine have ever grown and lacquered with a startling shade of red, and blond hair that defied description. It was crinkled and seemed to be everywhere from high above her head to almost as far as each shoulder. "I'm Arlene Hopkins," the woman said, extending her hand.

"Chris Bennett. Thank you for seeing me on such short notice."

"We were all devastated by Natalie's disappearance. Anything we can do to help, we will."

"Can you tell me how you came to hire Natalie?"

"We were just starting up and we needed a core staff. We ran an ad in the *Times* and she answered it. We didn't have a personnel department or recruiters or anything very professional at the time. We just let our guts tell us what to do. She was interviewed and she was hired."

"I wonder if you could show me the letter she wrote, her resume, letters of recommendation she sent, anything at all that you have."

Arlene Hopkins stared at me as though I had made some terrible faux pas. I looked at her with confusion, wondering if I had inadvertently offended her.

"I'm afraid that's impossible," she said finally.

"I really need—"

"I understand it might be useful to you. It's just that we don't have that material anymore."

"You've disposed of it?"

"When we opened the shop we didn't have two nickels to rub together. We had pencils and paper and an old file cabinet from my mother's basement. All those original records were on paper and very space-consuming. When we moved here last year, we threw out everything that hadn't been put on computer, especially for employees that were long gone. Payroll data is on computer, of course, but I don't know how helpful that would be for you."

Not very helpful at all. "Do you have any recollection of where she worked before she came here?"

She smiled, her lipsticked mouth a perfect replica of the nail polish shade. "I can hardly remember where I worked before I came here."

"Is there anything at all you can tell me?" I asked, feeling that I had really reached the end of the line rather soon with little to show for my day's work.

"She was an excellent secretary, more like everyone's assistant at the beginning, and we were sorry to lose her. I believe we sent her a very nice wedding present."

"Did she have any friends in the office?"

"She's been gone for two years. Most of our staff has been hired since then. But feel free to ask around. And if you hear anything about Natalie, I'd like to know."

I stood and offered her my hand. "Thank you. I will."

Halfway down the hall I ran into the receptionist, who had obviously been called to get me. She took me to a room where several people sat at computers or word processors, and told them to talk to me.

It wasn't very fruitful. Most of them had been hired after Natalie left; one had known her briefly and knew only that she was leaving to get married. But the last one, a man about my age who worked in very casual clothes, said he had known Natalie for a year or more.

"Did you ever talk?"

"Sure. It's a friendly office."

"She tell you anything about herself? Where she was from? Boyfriends, girlfriends?"

"There was only one boyfriend that I remember, and she left to marry him."

"Other friends? Relatives?"

"There was a girl in the office she was friendly with, Susan something, but she left before Natalie did."

There was a nameplate on his worktable that said STEVE. "I'm almost at a dead end, Steve. If there's anything you can think of—"

"It was an office friendship. We had a cup of coffee together, lunch once in a while. We didn't date, we didn't see each other after work. I liked her. She was peppy and upbeat. I'm neither one of those things. If she had sisters and cousins and aunts, she never talked about them."

I took the ring of keys out of my bag and put them in front of him. "Were those Natalie's?"

"I don't know." He picked them up and looked at them, then got up and walked away. "Come with me," he said, looking back. "We moved here last summer and a lot of old stuff was thrown out, the stuff H and J started with. But a few of the desks from the original office were bought new, and they came along. I think one of them was Natalie's."

I followed him to a small office on the hall that led to Arlene Hopkins's big office. The door was open, but no one was inside. "I think this was hers. Let's give it a try." He put one of the small keys in the keyhole in the top center drawer. "Fits like a glove. Want to try it?"

I turned the key to lock, then back to unlock, the drawer. As I did so, the occupant of the office came in. Steve explained and the new man seemed unfazed.

"Was anything of hers in the desk when you inherited it?" I asked.

"There was just the usual junk. I cleaned it out and threw everything away. Besides, I think someone else used it for a while before I got it. I've only been here a year."

Steve and I went back to his work station. At least I knew now the keys actually belonged to Natalie. I wrote my name and phone number on a piece of paper and gave it to him. "Call me collect," I said, "if you think of anything."

He looked at it. "What do you think happened to her?"

"I don't know. I suppose she was kidnapped, but I have no idea by whom or why."

"You think her husband did it?"

"Why do you say that?"

"Isn't that the way it usually is? They have a fight and he kills her? All the rest is just to prove to the world he's innocent."

"My instinct is that he didn't."

"Well, you've probably got better instincts than mine." He put the paper in his pocket. "Let me know if you turn anything up."

I was on my way down in the elevator when I remembered the voice on the phone when I had called for the appointment. I hadn't met anyone who sounded like that woman. When the elevator stopped on the ground floor, I took it right back up again.

"Forget something?" the receptionist said as I walked in.

"There was someone I wanted to talk to, but I didn't meet her, the woman I spoke to on the phone."

She looked baffled. "You talked to me."

"It was someone else."

"Arlene Hopkins?"

"I don't think so."

"I'm afraid I can't help you."

"Can I talk to Steve again, please?"

"Steve who?"

"In the word-processing room."

"He just left."

I hate when people think they can put something over on me. "I just talked to him five minutes ago," I said.

"And he left right after you did. I'm surprised you didn't run into him at the elevator."

I knew how to get from where I was standing to the room where Steve had his work station, but I don't really have what it takes to do something like that when it's pretty clear I've been asked to leave. This was private property, after all, and I didn't think I had any right to be there if they didn't want me.

I left.

I rode down to the ground floor feeling irritable. My visit, now that it was over, seemed orchestrated. Arlene Hopkins had said the papers connected to Natalie's tenure had been destroyed only last year, after her disappearance. Why would they have done such a thing? And the people they had invited me to talk to, the ones working in the word-processing area—weren't there others in the agency who might have known Natalie? Why had I been steered only toward one group and kept carefully away from every-one else?

But what bothered me most of all was the voice on the phone when I called from Westchester. It hadn't been Arlene Hopkins, and as a partner, she wasn't likely to answer a phone without someone running interference. There had been a woman and she called Sandy while I hung on and then agreed to give me an appointment in an hour. Who was she and why couldn't I talk to her again?

I buttoned my coat in the lobby of the building and pulled on my gloves. A man in a hurry opened the door and held it for me. As I thanked him, I thought I heard my name called. I looked around on the street and saw no one.

"Chris Bennett?"

I turned toward the building. The man named Steve was just coming out, still in his shirtsleeves. "Steve?"

"Glad I caught you. I missed your elevator going down and I must have lost you in the street. Did you go back inside?"

"I forgot something and went back up. Let's go inside. You must be freezing."

"I thought of something right after you left." He was rubbing his bare hands together as though he had the first stages of frostbite. "Who else did you talk to besides our group?"

"Arlene Hopkins."

"That all?"

"That was it."

"I don't know if they have something to hide or what, but Arlene is Miss Fixit around here. You've heard of the glass ceiling? She's the iron wall. You talk to Wormy?"

"Who?"

"The office manager, Eleanor Wormholtz. She's kind of a charter member of H and P. Wormy knows everything. Wormy knows things that haven't happened yet."

"I wonder if she's the one I talked to when I called for an appointment."

"She gets the overflow sometimes. Besides, she has brains. The girl at the door gave hers up a long time ago."

"How can I talk to this Eleanor Wormholtz? When I asked the receptionist if I could talk to the woman who answered the phone, she said she had. She hadn't."

"They're really giving you a runaround. You mind if I give Wormy your number?"

"I'd be grateful if you would. I don't suppose you know her number?"

"I can't do that."

"I understand. I appreciate your help."

"I told you. I liked Natalie. I want you to find her."

We shook hands and he went off to the elevators.

8

I don't think I ever quite appreciated the beauty of Friday night until I married. There are no classes, there are two days in the offing without work, there is the chance to be lazy, to talk, to do absolutely nothing. Of course, we don't always get to indulge ourselves over the weekend, but at least the opportunity is there.

Jack came home just about when the chicken and rosemary and garlic fragrances were becoming intense and when the thermometer indicated I had a dinner ready to be eaten.

"Got you some stuff from the file," he said after we kissed. "It won't make you jump up and down."

"Tell me."

"They did a sixty-one on Natalie's disappearance two days after Thanksgiving."

"What's that?"

"It's the initial report of a crime or an incident which may become a crime. The missing persons report would start with a sixty-one. They wouldn't do that on Thanksgiving because in most of these cases the person turns up pretty quickly. The cop he stopped after the parade would have told him to call home, go to the car, hang around and wait, that kind of thing. Most uniformed cops have had this kind of case before, boyfriend loses girlfriend, girlfriend loses boyfriend. If it had been a child at the parade, it would have been a different story. In this case, if she didn't show up eventually, they'd suggest he come into the precinct and talk to a detective, which is what he did. He brought a photograph with him and they did a send-around."

"Which is?"

"They make copies and send the picture to all the hospitals in the city to make sure she isn't in one listed as a Jane Doe, you know, a woman brought in without identification. Maybe she fainted and got picked up and taken somewhere and she hasn't come out of it yet. Detectives are just as anxious to get a missing persons case closed with results as any other crime case. There's a handwritten note that Sandy was asked to bring in all her prescriptions. There was only one, a cough medicine she'd gotten about a month earlier. So I'd guess she was in pretty good health."

"I assume there were no positive responses from the hospitals."

"Nothing. The detective working on the case, a Tony DiRoma, went out to New Jersey himself and talked to the neighbors."

"Because he figured Sandy killed her."

"It's what happens, Chris. But he seemed pretty satisfied they had a good marriage. No one ever saw her with bruises, no one heard screams or arguments, she always looked happy, chatted with neighbors."

"I'm glad to hear it. What did DiRoma do in New York?"

"He talked to the doormen on Central Park West and asked if they'd seen anything, and the answer was a pretty conclusive no."

"Did he go to her last job?"

"Hopkins and Something? He called."

"He didn't go and talk to people?"

"She hadn't worked there for a while, Chris. They told him everybody liked her and no one knew anything."

"Did he go to the building she lived in before she was married?"

"Doesn't look like it. He'd need a reason for that, Chris."

"Someone there might have known her."

"So what? They're not looking to write a life story, they're looking for a kidnapper. Anyway, DiRoma was transferred to another job about six months later and a new detective took over, Evelyn Hogan."

"Interesting. She do anything?"

"Looks like she did. She reviewed the file and checked up on Sandy. What did you do to this chicken?"

"What do you mean?" I asked in terror.

"It's great. I thought you said you couldn't roast a chicken."

"Melanie said anyone could roast a chicken and she told me exactly what to do."

"It's fantastic. You used rosemary."

I glowed. "Isn't it a wonderful smell?"

"Yup, I think I'm going to retire as chief cook in this house."

"Please don't do that."

"Competition's getting pretty keen around here."

"I'll go back to convent stew."

He looked at me and I laughed. The food at St. Stephen's had been very good, cooked by nuns who enjoyed cooking and who had their specialties.

"Well, I wasn't planning on giving up my title just yet."

"What's for tomorrow?"

"I'll think about it tonight. Haven't had lamb for a while, have we?"

"That sounds good. Want to hear my day?"

"I'm all ears."

I went through my morning conversation with Sandy and then what Susan Hartswell had told me, omitting her food and drink concerns. He raised his eyebrows when I said

Natalie had confided she might be pregnant and Sandy had likely not been told. Then I went through the Hopkins and Jewell episode. When I got to the missing personnel files, he interrupted for the first time.

"That really stretches the limits of credibility," he said. "It's not as if she'd been gone for twenty-five years. It was only a year or two. And you said it's a small place. How many files could they have accumulated?"

"Is any of the stuff I asked for in the police file?"

"None of it. But again, they weren't interested in her work history."

"And they started out with a bias," I said.

"Probably."

I told him the rest and I watched his interest increase as I came to the end, the woman I couldn't talk to because she didn't exist, the man named Steve following me out of the building.

"So they're holding something back," Jack said.

"They are, I'm sure of it. But what? Why would they dispose of her personnel records? What on earth could they say that Hopkins and Jewell wouldn't want me to know? Or wouldn't want the police to know?"

"Beats me. But I think you're on to something."

"Should I tell Sandy Natalie may have been pregnant?"

"I thought you were the half that decided moral issues."

I had done it before, deciding to withhold information from a family when that information could only cause them anguish and could cause no one any good. But in this case I was "working" for a "client" and I felt an obligation to keep him informed.

"Did Detective Evelyn Whatever find anything in her check of Sandy?" I asked.

"No evidence he ever beat either of his wives. His ex doesn't love him, but she doesn't seem to hate him either. The people who work for him like him. At least they didn't tell horror stories about him. Some seemed pretty fond of

him. I've copied some of the Fives for you to look at."
"Fives" are D.D.5s, Detective Division sheets on which information is typed for a case file. "If he did it, there were none of the usual calls to the police complaining of battering."

"So he isn't a suspect."

"Not officially, but I gotta believe DiRoma and Hogan started out with suspicions."

"He lives in New Jersey. Did the New Jersey police cooperate?"

"Looks like it. It's a pretty small town and they're pretty sure nothing was going on that they didn't hear about."

"I've got to talk to this Wormy woman, Jack. She must know something."

"Something they don't want you to find out."

I had a brief conversation with Sandy Gordon that night, telling him the keys were definitely Natalie's.

"So you've made progress on your first day," he said enthusiastically. "That's great."

"I have a couple of other things to check, and you'll hear from me when I've done it. By the way, did a woman from Hopkins and Jewell call you this afternoon for permission for me to make inquiries?"

"The office manager, yes. I didn't get her name, but I told her you had carte blanche. They didn't give you any trouble, did they?"

"No trouble, but I'd like to go back and talk to some other people there. Did your detective get anything useful from them?"

"Only that Natalie was one of the first people they hired, that they were sorry to see her go, they liked her, that kind of stuff. No one seemed to have a grudge, there were no stories about fights or arguments."

"Pretty much what I heard. OK, I'll be in touch."

* * *

I woke up Saturday morning thinking of my father. Jack had already awakened, and when I went out into the hall, I smelled coffee. It's a great smell to wake up to, and I got downstairs quickly so we could eat together. I had bought a couple of banana walnut muffins for breakfast, and they were already cut in half and waiting for me in the toaster oven. "We have anything on for this weekend?" he asked when we were sitting down.

"Nothing. I knew last Sunday would be completely taken up, so I thought I'd keep this weekend free. Got much work?"

"The usual. I'll leave it for tomorrow. Anything you want to do?"

"A couple of things. How determined are you not to go to New York today?"

"For you, love, I'll make the sacrifice. What's your pleasure?"

"How long is it since you've been to the Metropolitan Museum of Art?"

"Don't embarrass me. It sounds like today's a good day to do it."

"And maybe we can take a look at Sixty-fourth Street."

"The Statue of Liberty."

"Mind?"

"Haven't been up that way for a long time. How about we have dinner in the city and I'll cook tomorrow?"

"Sounds good."

"Where'd you get these great muffins?"

We drove to the city in the afternoon and parked at the museum. I was amazed at the crowds. People of every age, together, alone, in families, were piling in and out of the front doors as we entered. Like everyone who works in the city, I wore sneakers with my suit, carrying my good shoes in a bag to wear later. The city has taken on the look of a giant track meet these days, all those sneakered feet moving quickly along the pavement, ready to broad-jump at each corner. For me it was comfort, not speed, that dictated my footwear.

We looked at some of the classic paintings first, the old masters of the Dutch and Flemish schools, walking through packed galleries with the Saturday crowd. The people were nearly as interesting as the paintings. Some kept up a running commentary, some stared in silence, some moved toward and away from a particular painting as though focusing a preset camera lens, waiting for the image to become clear by changing the distance. A woman nursed a baby on a bench, a man with a beard narrowed his eyes and cocked his head, a father directed his daughter how to look at a canvas and what to look for while the wife and mother moved away from them at her own pace. I heard Spanish and French and something that may have been Russian.

Finally we went back downstairs and found our way to the Egyptian wing.

"This where they met?" Jack asked.

"Somewhere around here."

"Shall I move away and see if you can re-create history?"

"No, thank you."

"Sometimes I feel guilty that I deprived you of becoming part of the New York singles scene by preempting you."

"I'm not sure I would have survived it."

"Got something against one-night stands?"

"Lots."

It was a nice place to spend a Sunday afternoon, or a Saturday. I had read about the Egyptian buildings being moved, stone by stone, from their place of origin to be reassembled in this new home. I felt good that these antiquities had found a congenial home where they would be taken care of with the love and appreciation they deserved.

I moved to the side to watch the people rather than the exhibit. You could almost pick out the hopefuls at first glance, young women and not so young women in ones and twos, the twos sometimes together, sometimes separating, women dressed almost deliberately casually, their clothes a carefully thought out statement. They touched their hair frequently, moving toward single men with a practiced subtlety they must have been sure passed for chance. I watched one woman initiate a conversation with a bearded man who seemed less than interested. After a perfunctory smile, he moved away and she stayed, her eyes fixed on the Egyptian antiquity, looking for all the world like Natalie Miller. A few minutes later she turned and left the room.

"Maybe she should take up skiing," Jack said.

"Doesn't anyone do anything for the sake of the thing?"

"Sure. You and me."

"What a way to live."

We drove through Central Park to the west side of Manhattan and Jack zigged and zagged his way south so that we were able to enter Sixty-fourth from Broadway. Jack pulled over to the side and double-parked. "Want to look around?"

"Come with me?"

"Sure."

He put a plastic-covered police marker plate in the window, made sure the cars at the curb could get out, and joined me on the sidewalk. "You think she lived in one of these buildings?"

"Either that or she lived on Sixty-fourth farther west, toward the river. Why else would we have met her on that corner?" I nodded toward the corner of Central Park West.

"So you could have the pleasure of seeing the Statue of Liberty."

"I hadn't thought of that."

"Any idea how you're going to move on this?"

"I think I'll have to start where my father worked. It was

a place in downtown Manhattan. And I want to look through the stuff my aunt has in our basement."

"I've been afraid to ask you what's down there."

I wasn't surprised. The basement was an accumulation of a lifetime or two of acquisitions, my aunt's and my mother's. When my mother died and the house was sold, Aunt Meg took whatever was left and put it in her basement, assuming I would want those things at some point. It seemed the point was now.

"There are probably things my mother couldn't throw away, and I hope to find some photo albums down there. I promise I'll throw out everything I can."

"I'm not pushing."

"But it would be nice to have an emptier basement."

We had reached the corner of Central Park West, the Ethical Culture Society on the south corner. I remembered people lining the sidewalks and the stairs of buildings, hanging out of windows in apartment houses, standing on narrow balconies, all to see the parade. We had always stood on this corner, as close as we could squeeze to the curb.

"What do you remember about her?" Jack asked.

"Very little beyond her existence. But they knew each other. They smiled at each other. She knew my name."

"Did she have a name?"

"If she did, it didn't stick with me."

We turned back and I looked up at the statue, wondering how long it had been there. At the corner where Sixty-fourth crossed Broadway and Ninth Avenue in the jumble of streets, we could see some of the buildings of Lincoln Center.

"There are apartment houses on the far side of Lincoln Center," Jack said. "Over on Amsterdam Avenue."

"I remember." I'd been up this way before. "Probably thousands of people living there."

"Probably."

"Something'll turn up," I said.

"My wife the optimist. We done here?"

"I think so."

He looked at his watch. "How about I take you to a cop bar to kill some time before our dinner reservation?"

"A place where cops go after work?"

"Right. Not much class but a good place to unwind. Let's get rid of the car first. There's a place I remember around here from my early days."

It was nice for me to make a connection with Jack's life before he met me. He's been to St. Stephen's several times and met the nuns I grew up among, but aside from a small number of his friends on the job, I knew less of his early life than he knew of mine.

I kept my ears open while we sat at a table and had a drink, hoping to hear cop talk, department gossip, some clever political scheming, but it was all pretty mundane and I wasn't sure the voices I overheard even belonged to cops. But it was fun and relaxing and we did our own talking. About twenty minutes before our reservation, we left and took a leisurely walk down Broadway in the dark.

9

When the phone rang at five after twelve on Sunday, I had the feeling that the caller had waited till noon for the sake of politeness.

"Is this Christine Bennett?"

"Yes it is."

"This is Steve Carlson from Hopkins and Jewell. I hope I didn't wake you up."

I had already been to mass with Gene and taken him back to Greenwillow. "I've been up for hours."

"I talked to Wormy yesterday. I called her at home. There's something weird going on."

It's the kind of news that gives my skin a prickle. "Tell me about it."

"Wormy knows everything about that shop. The legend is she was the first person hired when H and J opened their doors. She may even be related to one of them in some way, I'm not sure. But she knows as much about what goes on there as H and J do. Maybe more."

"Then she's a good person to talk to."

"She won't talk to you."

"Did she say why?"

"She said it wasn't any of her business, that if Arlene spoke to you, what else was there to say?"

"I see. Well, I thank you for trying, Steve. Maybe on Monday I'll go down and ask to see her."

"I'll give you her phone number."

That surprised me. He had said on Friday that he wouldn't. "That's very nice of you."

He dictated the number. From the area code I could tell she lived in Brooklyn, Queens, or Staten Island. "She has a husband and a couple of kids that are probably late teens or twenties. I'd appreciate if you wouldn't say straight out that I gave you the number, but she'll probably guess."

"Do you have any sense of what she could be hiding or what she could be reluctant to talk about?"

"Not in the slightest. Natalie came to work in the morning and left in the evening like the rest of us. As far as I know, she did a hell of a good job."

"I appreciate your help, Steve."

I thought about it all day. I didn't relish talking to a hostile informant who would prefer not to be called at home. After a light lunch Jack went upstairs to the little bedroom we had fixed up as a study, so I went down to the basement and started looking through the dozens of boxes that were my inheritance. The ones with my mother's name on them were separated and pushed into a corner. I hadn't thought to bring a knife with me, so I untied the rope on one that said SCRAPBOOKS AND ALBUMS on the top.

It was an afternoon of nostalgia and even a few tears. All my baby pictures were there, my parents looking like a couple of kids, I like a bundle of blankets. There was the house I grew up in, Gene and I playing in a sandbox, Aunt Meg and Uncle Willy, lots of smiles. Events I remembered were recorded, my graduation from grade school, this time without my father present, a birthday party we had celebrated at a bowling alley and then later at home with cake and ice cream, a school play in which I had had a substantial part. There were no pictures of any Thanksgiving Day parade, but I had not recalled my father taking a camera with him. Not all the people in the pictures were identifiable, but I was reasonably sure none was the mystery woman of the parade.

Deep in the box was a framed picture of my parents on their wedding day, probably the only existing picture of the occasion. I did not remember ever seeing an album or hearing of a large wedding, but they were dressed as a traditional bride and groom. I rubbed the glass with the bottom of my sweater and blew away dust. It would be nice to keep this where I could look at it, upstairs in one of the bedrooms.

A box a little smaller than a shoe box held many pictures of varying size and quality, most of them unfamiliar to me. Both sets of my grandparents were there in formal, unsmiling portraits as well as some more casual ones. Many pictures had dates and names on the back, but many others did not. Who was Joe Formica? Who was Mrs. Elsevere? I went through them one by one, turning them over into the top of the box to keep the order the same. There was my mother as a child with three unidentified children. There was my father with my aunt Meg—they were brother and sister—as little children at the beach, in the country, plowing happily through snow.

I was sitting under a naked lightbulb, on an old wooden folding chair I had found down there, renewing my family relationships. From time to time the furnace would go on and then, some time after, switch off. After I'd been downstairs for a long time, I heard the hot water heater go on and I figured Jack must be taking a shower, but I was as transfixed, as hooked, as I ever get and I kept turning over picture after picture, no longer looking for anything or anyone special, just looking with interest and nostalgia and an aching sense of being too late. Why had I not asked Aunt Meg years ago, during the time I was visiting regularly, if such pictures existed, if she could help me put a name or some kind of identity on them? It had not occurred to me.

I had been in my twenties and I had looked forward, not back, and now I was sorry.

Dimly I heard my name called and I started out of my reverie.

"Chris? You home?"

"I'm down here, Jack."

The door to the basement opened. "Down where?"

"I'm looking at old pictures."

"You been down there all afternoon?"

"I guess."

He came down the stairs. "You like spiders or something? I could have carried this stuff up and you could have sat in the living room."

"It was better this way." I stood up and took the framed wedding picture. Then I pulled the chain on the lightbulb and followed Jack up to civilization.

He had put lamb shanks in a pot with wine and herbs and vegetables before his shower, but cooking odors only go up and I had been unaware. He poured me a glass of sherry and took some of his favorite Scotch for himself.

"Find anything?" he asked.

"Lots and lots of stuff but no mysterious woman. I didn't find any papers anywhere. As I remember, there are baptismal certificates and birth certificates in the box in the bank. I was a co-owner with Aunt Meg and I just kept it after she died."

"The woman probably worked with your father and came out to say hello at the parade."

"I'll find out. I'll go down during the week. Right now I have to decide whether to call this Wormholtz woman at home."

"I'd say go for it."

"That's my feeling, too. I hope she doesn't hang up on me."

"Want some Scotch to stiffen your resolve?"

"The sherry's fine, thanks. It's mellowed me."

"Ah, Christine Bennett Brooks, normally the world's most unmellow woman."

I smiled and went to the kitchen to make my call.

"Do I know you?" The voice was the one I remembered, firm, tough, unbending.

"My name is Christine Bennett, Mrs. Wormholtz. We spoke on Friday."

"Refresh my memory."

"I called Hopkins and Jewell to make an appointment. You got me one."

"If you say so. What are you doing calling me at home?"

"I'm working on something very important and I think you can help me."

"I work at the office five long days a week. You can reach me there any time from—"

"Mrs. Wormholtz, this isn't advertising business. This is life and death. Natalie Miller Gordon disappeared over a year ago and I am trying to find out what happened to her. The receptionist at H and J refused to let me speak to you, and I know you can help me."

"That's who you are."

"That's who I am, yes. Please, give me a few minutes. Please try to help me."

"What do you want to know?"

"Did you know Natalie?"

"I know every person who's ever worked for H and J including the cleaning crew."

"Did you know her personally? Did you ever talk to her? Did you have lunch with her?"

"A qualified yes to all three questions. We talked. She seemed like a nice enough person. I knew when she met the man she eventually married. I had lunch with her occasionally when we had a business party and a group went together. We weren't friends. We didn't meet after hours."

"Did you like her?"

She took a breath before she said, "I liked her."

"Do you know where she worked before she came to H and J?"

"No idea."

"I understand you're the office manager."

"That's right."

"Can you tell me why you got rid of the material in Natalie's personnel file?"

"What material?"

"Her references, her records of past employment—"

"Slow down, Ms. Bennett. Who exactly told you I got rid of that stuff?"

No one had. "I was led to believe—"

"By whom?" she interrupted.

"Arlene Hopkins said—"

"Arlene Hopkins never told you I removed any papers from that file because I didn't and she knows it."

"She said a lot of files were thinned out to save space when you moved to your present location."

"No doubt that's true. I didn't do any thinning. And I definitely didn't do any thinning of that file."

"Do you have any idea who did?"

"I have an opinion on almost everything."

There was little doubt that was true. "Will you tell me?" I was starting to feel like a trial lawyer, phrasing a new question to elicit each molecule of information.

"I will not. I'm the office manager, not the president of the company. It's not my place to tell you something Arlene Hopkins won't tell you."

"How am I going to find out?"

"Talk to Marty Jewell."

"Mr. Jewell?" I had half expected Jewell to be another woman. "How can I get to see him?"

"I'll arrange it. When do you want to come?"

"Tomorrow."

"Be there at ten. You may have to wait a while, but I'll see to it he gives you your fifteen minutes."

"I'll be there. Thank you, Mrs. Wormholtz."

"Good afternoon."

10

The receptionist recognized me and gave me a plastic smile. Then she made a phone call and said, "She's here."

I waited a long time. Maybe I was being taught a lesson; maybe they were as busy as they seemed. People came in with deliveries, arrived for appointments that were kept pretty punctually, people left. At ten to eleven a woman appeared in the reception area.

"Miss Bennett?"

I stood up. "Yes."

"Come with me."

She was fortyish, thick in the middle, had dark hair she had forgotten to brush for several days, and she was dressed in a black skirt and blouse of an unidentifiable fabric that did nothing to enhance her looks, but she didn't seem to care. She never introduced herself, just started to walk briskly, and I followed because I had been promised fifteen minutes of someone's time and I didn't want to waste any of it walking.

Jewell had the other corner office and he was on the phone when we got there. The woman stood in the doorway till he hung up, then said, "This is Christine Bennett."

"Thanks, Wormy," Mr. Jewell said with a sincere smile. "Come on in." As I entered, he turned back to her. "You take care of that Goodman thing, OK?"

There was no acknowledgment, but I assumed her silence meant she was about to do some taking care of.

"Please sit down, Miss Bennett. Can I take your coat?" He rushed to make me comfortable.

As surprised as I had been to see Arlene Hopkins in her pin-striped suit and hair, I was equally surprised to see Martin Jewell. He looked as informal as his partner was formal, wearing a tieless white shirt and no jacket, the sleeves rolled up a couple of turns. He had a round face that at rest looked cordial and relaxed, ready to spring a joke on a willing listener.

"I understand you're looking into Natalie's disappearance."

"That's right. I'm not a professional, but I've had some experience, and her husband asked me if I'd try to find out what happened to her."

"It was shocking," he said. "She was crazy about him. You couldn't talk to her five minutes without hearing Sandy this and Sandy that. I don't know how she could have done it."

"Done what?"

He looked a little confused. "Walked away from him like that."

"Why do you think she did?"

He shrugged. He was sitting behind his desk again, a desk as cluttered as his partner's was empty. "What else could have happened? I heard they went to the Thanksgiving Day parade and she walked away."

"You think she just kept walking?"

"It's not very likely someone grabbed her, is it?"

"It's too soon for me to say what is and isn't likely. Do you have any idea where she would have gone if she ran away?"

"Not a clue."

"Do you know where she was from?"

"She was living in New York when she worked here. I couldn't tell you whether she was a native or came from somewhere else. She didn't sound like a New Yorker, but maybe she was from upstate."

"Was she friendly with anyone in the office?"

"Uh, yes, there was someone. Susan, I think. Susan left before Natalie got married. I don't know where she is now."

"Susan Diggins," I said.

"That's the one."

"Anyone else?"

"We all knew her. I just wouldn't call anyone else a friend of hers, but I could be wrong. I don't always know what goes on after hours."

"What concerns me is that information from Natalie's file seems to be missing."

"Have you seen the file?"

"No. Arlene Hopkins told me."

"What did she say happened to it?"

When someone starts asking me the questions, I get the feeling they're checking out my source, perhaps trying to shape their own answers and not put themselves or anyone else on the spot. "Can you tell me what happened to those papers?"

"Which papers exactly?"

"Her references, her record of previous employment, her education. I would imagine you wouldn't hire someone off the street if you were a new business with limited funds to throw around."

He gave me a smile. "You know, that's exactly what we did. We put a very clever ad in the *Times*—we did the ad ourselves—and we did the interviewing and we made all the decisions. We were pretty much our own personnel department, and to tell you the truth, in the old office, we kind of policed the grounds, too, if you know what I mean. We couldn't afford a cleaning service, so it was do it yourself or live knee-high in dust."

I don't know why I liked him, but I did. He had managed for several minutes now not to answer my question, but there was something very appealing about his manner, as there was something very forbidding about Arlene Hopkins's. "But she wrote to you applying for the job and she supplied you with references," I said, not asking.

"I guess she must have."

"And those papers are missing from her file."

"Yes."

"What happened to them, Mr. Jewell?"

"They disappeared a long time ago," he said.

Finally. "How long ago?"

"Years."

"Can you tell me the circumstances?"

"Wormy was—that's Mrs. Wormholtz, who brought you in here—she was looking for something in the personnel files and she found Natalie's almost empty. All the things you mentioned were gone."

"So there had been records in the file."

"There had been records."

"Was Natalie working here at that time or had she left?"

"She was working here."

"Did you talk to her about it?"

"Wormy did."

"And?"

"And Natalie was upset."

"Did she have any idea why someone would want to raid her file?"

"No idea at all."

"Was anyone else's file raided?"

"I think Wormy made a spot check and found things pretty much in order. She's a great office manager and she really took it personally that her files were incomplete."

"Did you ask Natalie to replace any of the missing papers?"

"Wormy probably asked her. I think she said she'd try to get copies, but I don't think she ever did."

"Was there evidence of a break-in before this happened?"

"We've never had a break-in."

"Who interviewed Natalie before she came to work here?"

"I did. I told you, we—"

"I understand," I said, sparing myself a repetition. "Only you?"

"She was going to be my secretary. Arlene didn't have to approve. I'm sure Wormy talked to her, too."

I hadn't realized that Natalie had been Martin Jewell's secretary. "Then Natalie worked only for you?"

"Listen, we opened in disarray and we progressed to chaos. Nominally she was my secretary, but she did work for anyone who needed her. Like Wormy. Natalie could do anything."

"Did Arlene Hopkins have someone like that working for her?"

"She found someone, yeah."

I was getting strange feelings of incomplete answers and withheld information. "Was Natalie still your secretary when she left to get married?"

"You know, our whole present structure is different. It's evolved a lot from those early days. Natalie hadn't been my private secretary for a long time and I don't really have one now. We don't need one anymore, now that we've got a whole pool of people."

"Mr. Jewell, who do you think took those documents out of the file?"

"I don't know."

"Who had access to the personnel files?"

"All four of us did, Arlene, Natalie, Wormy, of course, and me. We were like charter members of a club."

"So any of the four of you could have stolen those documents?"

"I guess so. Or someone hired later who got into Wormy's office while she was out of it."

"Why would anyone do that?"

"Maybe there was something there someone didn't want us to know."

"Like what?"

"Like who she worked for before she came here, but don't ask me why because I don't know."

"Or what high school she went to or where she used to live."

"You can make it anything you want. I don't know what was in that file. I looked at it once, maybe five years ago when I interviewed Natalie, and I never looked again." He glanced at his watch and I knew I had used up my promised fifteen minutes, and then some.

I wrote my name, address, and phone number on a piece of paper and handed it to him.

"I know the drill," he said. "If I think of anything, you'll hear from me."

"Would you mind if I talked to Mrs. Wormholtz?" I asked.

"I wouldn't mind at all. She probably remembers a lot more than I do. I think she sends birthday cards to everyone who works here. Shall I call her?"

"I'd appreciate it." I got up and took my coat off the hook while he telephoned. At least he was letting me talk to Wormy. Arlene Hopkins had done her best to keep us apart. It had to be Hopkins who had prevented me from talking to Wormy last Friday.

"She's on her way." He was on his feet, extending his hand. "Look, anything I can do to help, let me know. Natalie was one of us, we all liked her, it took three people to replace her, and we'd all like to know what happened to her."

"I'll keep you posted."

There was a knock on the door and Wormy came in. "Right this way," she said, sparing no extra syllables.

I followed.

11

Her office was windowless, perhaps to give her more wall space. It was not a place for a claustrophobic. Old-fashioned metal file cabinets stood side by side, effectively covering the walls from the floor to about five feet above it. On top of some lay stacks of unfiled folders; on others there were photographs and objects that looked like the handiwork of children. I sat in the single extra chair and Wormy plopped into her desk chair with a sigh.

"What can I tell you?" she said.

"When did you come to work for Hopkins and Jewell?"

"Am I on trial here?"

"No one's on trial, Mrs. Wormholtz. I'm just trying to organize my information into a rough chronology."

"My mother is a cousin of Marty Jewell's mother. We've known each other all our lives. I had a lot of experience running business offices, and Marty convinced me to leave a very good job and come to work for him. I was reluctant, but he was very persuasive. I've never regretted it. I came to work the day they opened their agency."

"So you were there when Natalie Miller came for her interview."

"I set the interviews up. They advertised before they moved into their office. The responses went to a box number. I read them, discussed them with Arlene and Marty, and called the candidates to set up appointments."

"Do you remember where Natalie was working when she applied for the job?"

"Somewhere in midtown. Maybe a law office, maybe another ad agency. I have a good memory, but frankly, that's not the kind of thing that sticks."

"Mr. Jewell said you interviewed Natalie. Do you remember doing that?"

"Very well. She came across as very personable, she had terrific references, she was willing to come in almost immediately, and what I liked about her most was that she said she couldn't start tomorrow because she had work to clean up at the old job and she couldn't leave them in the lurch. Maybe I'm old-fashioned, but honorable still means something to me."

It was the kind of comment that touched a sympathetic chord. "Was there a period of time that just the four of you worked for the agency?"

"Now that you mention it, yes, I think there was."

"When did Arlene Hopkins get her own private secretary?"

"I did her secretarial work at the beginning. I told Marty I couldn't do it for him because we knew each other so well. So he got Natalie, and Arlene got me. But we all did everything at the beginning. Arlene and Marty knew each other, they'd gotten a hefty account which was enough to get them going, but barely. They scrounged some used furniture, a typewriter, a box of number two pencils, and they opened up."

"It must have been fun," I said, some latent entrepreneurial spirit awakening in me.

"It was," she said with the first hint of a smile. "Those were great days. Every time a new account came to us, we'd holler and scream. We'd go out to dinner and celebrate. There was a lot of good feeling that went around, a sense that we were all in on the beginning of something wonderful."

"Is it possible that Arlene Hopkins removed the missing documents from Natalie's file?" I asked, hoping she would give a little now that she was feeling nostalgic.

She looked troubled. "It's possible," she said, "but I can't think why she would. When I say it's possible I mean that she had a key to the office, she could have come in early, gone through the files, taken what she wanted, and been at her desk by the time anyone else arrived. Or she could have stayed late."

"I assume everything you've said would apply to Mr. Jewell, too."

"Every word. Applies to me, too, but I didn't take anything."

"But those cabinets must have been locked."

"Miss Bennett, we were using hand-me-down everythings. There were locks with no keys, there were locks that didn't work. We felt that what was important was our clients' materials. We didn't want anyone breaking in and stealing our business and our ideas. Who would want a secretary's resumé? We saved the locks and keys for the stuff that had commercial value."

"You're sure it wasn't Mr. Gordon's detective who took those papers last year."

"They were missing when Natalie was still here. That's a couple of years ago. More. Those papers were missing a year or so after we opened up. I went to put her first evaluation in the file and I saw it was practically empty."

"Who else had the key to the office?"

"I did."

"And—?"

"Arlene and Marty."

"No one else?"

"No one else was entitled. You can't go giving out keys and hope to keep your office secure."

"Did you check any of the references in Natalie's file?"

"As a matter of fact, I did. She asked that I not call her

present employer—that's not unusual; people don't want their bosses to know they're looking for another job—so I called the one before that. I don't remember who they were, but their reference was glowing."

"Could Hopkins or Jewell have known Natalie's employer or former employer? Could there have been something between them that would provide a reason to remove their existence from Natalie's file?"

"You're asking me what's possible. Sure it's possible. Lots of things are possible."

She was right, of course. And if there was one item in the file someone didn't want on record, it would be smart to remove other things so no one would know which piece of paper was the object of the search. "So you think the documents were taken about a year after the agency opened and Natalie started working here."

"I didn't say that. I said I discovered they were missing a year later. They weren't files I checked very often. That stuff could have been taken the day after we hired her."

"I see." I hesitated a moment. "Do you get along well with Arlene Hopkins?"

"I get along the same with everyone. I do a spectacular job here as I've done in all my jobs. If I rub people the wrong way, they learn how to avoid me."

It sounded a little evasive, but she was talking about her employer, and I sensed this was a woman with a strong sense of loyalty. "What about Martin Jewell?"

"I've known Marty all my life and there isn't a straighter, more honest human being on the face of this earth."

There didn't seem to be any point in continuing that line of questioning, not with a woman for whom honorable meant something. "Are Hopkins and Jewell married?" I asked.

"What makes you ask that?"

Interesting answer. "Curiosity."

"They've never married," she said, a trifle nervously, I thought. "I mean they haven't married each other. Marty's married to someone else."

"But there's something between them," I suggested.

"Look, I'm here to answer questions about a missing woman and some missing papers, not about in-house sexual relationships. Ask Arlene if you want an answer to that."

"It's not the kind of question I can ask her, and besides, we didn't hit it off. Arlene tried to prevent me from speaking to you last Friday."

"Then ask Marty." She looked at her watch. "Is there anything else I can help you with? I have a full day's work ahead of me and only half a day to do it in."

"One last question. You said on the phone yesterday that you knew who took the papers. Who do you think that was?"

"I said I had an opinion. I don't know anything for sure." She got out of her chair and went to the most battered of the file cabinets, opened a drawer and pulled out a folder. "This is Natalie's personnel file."

I took it from her and looked inside. There was a sheet of paper dated about five years ago with notes written in ballpoint ink and signed MJ, phrases with opinions he must have jotted down during his initial interview with Natalie. Following that was a typed sheet with similar comments by EW. There was nothing from Hopkins, but there were three evaluation forms with comments by all three of the charter members of Hopkins and Jewell, good comments for the most part. The skimpiest were from Hopkins, the most detailed from Jewell. On the last one, done not long before Natalie left to be married, Hopkins noted that Natalie spent too much time on the phone. There was nothing else in the folder.

"Thank you very much for your candidness," I said, handing the folder back to her.

Then I left.

12

I stopped in the downstairs lobby and opened my subway map. I had checked the address of my father's office over the weekend and it hadn't changed. It was still in downtown Manhattan and I could pick up a train a couple of blocks from where I was to get there. I buttoned up and went out into the cold.

If the photographs had stirred up my emotions, approaching the place where my father had worked most of his adult life nearly made them explode. Much of downtown Manhattan has changed little since the turn of the century. Some old factories and warehouses have been torn down or converted to fashionable living quarters or have become artists' lofts, but this one was just as I remembered it, old, brick, solid, dirty, windows cracked or even boarded up. I had visited only a few times as a child, brought by my mother for occasions like a Christmas party or by my father once in a while, just to show me off. I had been treated like royalty, admired, complimented, hugged, and patted. Chocolates had materialized, cookies had been sent for. My father had glowed and my natural shyness had eventually given way to a feeling of comfort. I remember always going home with stories for my mother about this one and that one, sharing my cookies with her, telling her how everyone had liked my dress.

The street door was open and I climbed a steep flight of stairs to the second floor and walked inside. People were dressed in jeans instead of the more formal attire of a quarter century ago. One woman in a skirt and blouse asked if she could help me, and I said I was looking for a Mr. Jackman if he was still working there.

"Sure he's here. Can I ask you what your business is?"

"It's more personal than business. My father worked here for a long time."

"Come on in. He'll be glad to see you. I think he's having lunch at his desk today."

I had forgotten lunch, not unusual for me when I'm working on something. I considered leaving and coming back in half an hour, but she was already far ahead of me and I ran a couple of steps to catch up.

The office was the kind I remembered, windowed so you could see into it from the inside. But the man eating a sandwich at his desk was far too young to have been working here when my father had.

"Go on in. Can I get you a cup of coffee?"

"No, thanks." I went in and he stood and looked at me. "Do I know you?"

"I think your father knew my father. I'm Eddie Bennett's daughter."

"Eddie Bennett, I remember the name. My dad used to talk about him."

"I met your father a few times when I was a little girl. I'm Chris." I offered my hand and we shook.

"Pleased to meet you. What brings you down here today?"

"A couple of memories. I wonder if you could check something for me. I think there was a woman who worked here who lived on the west side in the Lincoln Center area that we used to meet when we went to the Thanksgiving Day parade. I don't remember her name, but I wanted to see her again."

"How old do you think she'd be?"

"I'd guess between sixty and seventy. I met her when I was five or six and not a very good judge of age."

"You want to wait while I ask?"

"If you don't mind."

"Be right back." He picked up the rest of his sandwich and left the office.

I went to the outside window and looked out onto the street. Places that don't change fascinate me. It must have something to do with the comfort of finding one's way, the way you do in a house you've lived in for years. Night or day, you know the position of every piece of furniture, every door, every board that creaks and rug that trips you up. I have heard people complain about returning to scenes of their childhood or their most memorable experiences and being overwhelmed with disappointment. Buildings are gone, replaced with steel and glass, not the substances of mortal memory. But here time had stopped. Perhaps in another twenty-five years and a huge input of money, this area might become gentrified, replaced, converted into a park. I would not think about that today.

"Got it," a voice behind me said, and I turned to see Mr. Jackman with a piece of paper in his hand.

"You do? Really?"

"Here she is, Betty Campbell. Name ring a bell?"

"I'm not sure."

He handed me the address. "Amsterdam Avenue, right near Lincoln Center."

"That's exactly what I thought." Well, not exactly, but one of the possibilities.

"Well, I hope you find her. She's retired, lives by herself, I think. Nice woman. Worked here a long time. Your father died quite suddenly, didn't he?"

"That's what I remember. I think they came for me at school one day. It was a heart attack."

"Shame. He was not only a nice guy, he was the kind of salesman everybody loves, customers and us. Man with the kind of sense of honor you don't find in a lot of young people nowadays. He was a gem."

"Thank you."

"Is your mother still alive?"

"Unfortunately no. She died a few years after he did."

"Well, you come from a nice family, Chris. You can be proud of them."

We reminisced for a few minutes more and then I left. One of the women came out of her office as I passed and said something about my father. She had known him only a couple of years but remembered him well. As I walked to the west side subway, I felt closer to my father than I had for years. Imagine a woman coming out to say a good word. It was a kindness I really appreciated, one that would stay with me.

I went down into the subway and rode uptown to find Betty Campbell.

I got off at Sixty-sixth Street, right under Lincoln Center for the Performing Arts, and made my way to the street level, not certain where I wanted to be. Once outside, I took my bearings and walked a block west to Amsterdam Avenue. On the west side of the street a group of redbrick apartment houses ran the length of several blocks, although no street went through them. They'd been dressed up with greenery, that is, trees that would be green in the spring. So much of New York is concrete and brick that it always makes me feel good to see vegetation in brown earth.

With a little difficulty I found the entrance with Betty Campbell's number and rang her bell. She answered in seconds with a loud "Hello?"

"Ms. Campbell, it's Christine Bennett. May I come up for a minute?" I find that a woman who gives her name is frequently welcome even without an explanation.

"Oh yes, they said you'd be coming." Then she buzzed. I pushed the door open, realizing someone had called—

rather intelligently, I thought—to say I might be on my way. The elevator was waiting and I rode up to the fourth floor. A door was open and a woman was looking out. "I'm Chris," I said as I walked toward her, keeping my disappointment out of my voice. As dim as my memory was, as unreliable as a child's perceptions may be, this could not have been the woman at the parade. She was too short even to be a finalist in the nonexistent competition, and age or disease had crippled her, hunching her shoulders.

"Come right in. They said you were Eddie Bennett's daughter. Nice man, Eddie Bennett. I remember you when you were little, all dressed up to see your daddy's office." She turned two locks and shuffled, using a cane, to the kitchen.

I followed, my heart feeling heavy at this woman's pain. "These look like nice apartments," I said.

"They're nice enough. Gotta watch yourself at night, though."

"That's true everywhere."

"Times have changed, haven't they? Cup of coffee?"

"No, thanks."

"Then let's sit in the living room." She shuffled her way there and sat in a big, worn chair, hooking the cane on the arm. "Sad when Eddie died. You must've been no more than a child."

"I was about eight."

"What a tragedy. Man taken away from his family like that."

"He left a good legacy, a lot of happy memories."

"Can't ask for more than that. Have a mint." She extended a glass dish of flat round chocolates toward me. They had sat on the little table next to her chair, her daily treat.

I took one and let it melt in my mouth, two images passing before my eyes, one the young Proust dipping his madeleines, the second an older Proust tasting them to bring back the past. It was as though I were visiting Dad again at the office in my new dress. "Have you lived here long?" I asked.

"Almost fifteen years. I was on the list before that. In New York, you wait for someone to die and hope your name comes up." She laughed. "I guess there are folks out there waiting for me to kick the bucket, but they've got a while to go. I feel real good."

"You sound good," I said honestly. "You sound like an energetic person."

"Well, I've always been that. Broke my hip last year but haven't let it keep me down."

"Where did you live before?"

"Oh, way uptown on the west side. It's all changed. I used to like to walk in Riverside Park when I was younger, but you wouldn't catch me going there now. Here I've got the subway close by and buses right outside."

"It's very convenient," I agreed. "When did you start working for Mr. Jackman?"

"Maybe thirty-five years ago. Probably more. I knew your father for a long time. He'd come in in the morning with a big smile and a nice word for everybody. 'How're you doin' today, Betty?' Always nice to see him."

It was as if each small addition to my archive of memories fleshed him out that much more. I could hear his voice saying the words, see the grin. "I want to ask you something kind of silly, Betty. Did you used to go to the Thanksgiving Day parade when my dad worked for Mr. Jackman?"

"Haven't been to the parade since I was a child. I watch it on the TV now. I don't like crowds. There's a mess of crowds for that parade."

"Tell me something. Did you know anyone who worked for Mr. Jackman who lived around here when my father worked there?"

"Who lived here? Let me see." She looked down at the

worn carpet at her feet. Her hair, which was black with deeply encroaching gray, was long and pulled back behind her head, gathered in a black velvet band. Her face was jowly and lined, bare of the slightest color. "A lot of them came from Brooklyn because you could take the old BMT into Manhattan in those days. That's gone now, you know. All those trains have letters on 'em, never know where you're going anymore. I used to come down on the Broadway line, same as what's at Lincoln Center. Where did Gloria live?" she asked, as though the answer would come from the air around us. "I'm wrong," she said, as though correcting a statement unspoken. "Gloria was this young, cute girl, but now I think of it, she lived in the Village. Dressed like she lived in the Village, too, long hair and those exotic clothes. She left maybe around the time Eddie died. Got another job."

"What color hair did she have?" I asked, although I knew the woman of my memory didn't look Villagey in any sense.

"Black as coal. Gloria, can't remember her last name."

"So you don't think anyone who worked there lived up on the west side."

"I don't think so, honey."

"What about old Mr. Jackman?"

"Oh, he always lived out in Queens, had a beautiful house, I heard." She made the adjective long and drawn out.

"Well, I guess that answers all my questions."

"Oh, don't go," she said. "Stay a while. It's good to have company, nice to have a young person to talk to. Tell me about yourself, what you're doing now."

I sat back in the chair and talked to her for the next half hour. Her eyes sparkled as we exchanged reminiscences and brought each other up to date on our lives. I had no recollection of ever meeting this woman before, but when I left she was someone who fitted into my life. After about

THE THANKSGIVING DAY MURDER 97

half an hour and two more mints, I said good-bye, went back downtown to retrieve my car, and drove home.

"Thanks for calling," Sandy Gordon said. "I've been waiting to hear from you."

"I expect I've gotten all I can from Hopkins and Jewell, and while there are some intriguing things, I don't see where they lead."

"Like what?"

"Did you know the documents in Natalie's personnel file were stolen or misplaced?"

"The detective said they didn't have much from before the time she worked for them. He saw her evaluations, which he said were very flattering."

"They are. But that's all there is. Whatever letter she wrote answering their ad, whatever references she sent or high school transcripts, they're all missing and no one has any idea who took them or why."

"Did they talk to Natalie about it?"

"Yes and she was upset."

"So what do you think?"

"I think there may have been some bad feelings between Arlene Hopkins and Natalie."

"Anything special make you feel that way?"

"Hopkins didn't want me talking to anyone except her. She had me steered to the word-processing pool, where only one person knew Natalie and he hadn't been there from the beginning."

"So you think they're keeping something from you."

"I think they tried. I probably found out more than Hopkins wanted me to know, but I don't know if I've got everything. And if I don't, I really don't know where else to look, except for Natalie's old apartment."

"When will you go there?"

"I teach tomorrow. It'll have to wait for Wednesday."

"You're doing fine, Chris. I mean that. I'm sure you're

on to something and you're a digger, I can see that. You'll find her. Need any more money?"

"Good heavens no. All it's going for is parking."

"Let me know when you run out."

I dropped a note to Arnold telling him about Hopkins and Jewell, my visit to my father's office, and what I intended to do next. If he had urgent work, I'd be glad to do it, but otherwise I seemed to have enough to occupy all my time.

13

We are both early risers and we do a lot more talking of substance in the morning when we're fresh than in the evening when Jack is exhausted from school and driving and my metabolism is running on empty. He didn't need to ask anything as we sat down to breakfast on Tuesday morning. I told him.

"So anyone who walked into this woman Wormy's office when she wasn't there could have stolen the stuff in the file," he said.

"Essentially yes. And she must have gone out to lunch sometimes, no matter how dedicated she was. If a person goes out to lunch, she'll be gone at least twenty minutes, and that's really cutting it short."

"But someone with a key could stay late and be safely alone."

"And both principals have keys, along with Wormy."

"What's the motivation for Arlene Hopkins to take the papers?"

"How's this? Natalie finds out something about Arlene that Arlene would like to keep quiet. Maybe she knows Natalie overheard a conversation she had with someone in her office or on the phone, or maybe Natalie fielded a call to Arlene that Arlene wished she hadn't. So she takes the documents one day looking for something in them she can use as a kind of blackmail."

"Now you're talking."

"It's even possible she didn't mean to keep them. She may only have wanted to look at them in the privacy of her office or at home. She takes them, planning to make copies or just look at them and return them, and by coincidence, in the short time they're gone, Wormy opens the file to put Natalie's first evaluation in it and finds it almost empty."

"Makes sense. Once Wormy lets others know there are papers missing, Arlene, or whoever took them, can't put them back."

"Right."

"But they're just as gone for your purposes as if they were taken to be destroyed."

"I know. And even if Arlene admitted she took them, what good would it do? They were probably destroyed four years ago or more."

"Sounds like you've got problems, sweetheart. I haven't had a course yet in rematerializing destroyed documents."

"Gosh," I said, "and I was really counting on you."

"You intend to push this woman a little?"

"I don't think I can. I found it a little hard to relate to her. She was wearing a pin-striped suit and hair out to here."

"That kind of woman used to do something to me."

I laughed. "Don't tell me what."

"So you're telling me it's a dead end."

"I still have Natalie's old apartment house to visit. Of course, she hasn't lived there for a couple of years. I'll go in tomorrow."

"Where did she live?"

I went to the dining room where I'd left my notes. "Looks like Greenwich Avenue."

"Ah, the Village. Narrow streets, old buildings, the artsy crowd. Gets a little rowdy down there on weekends now, but it's nice during the day. Pretty. Find yourself a nice little restaurant and have lunch at Sandy's expense. Bet you haven't been doing that."

I thought with some embarrassment of my lunchless day yesterday. "I haven't."

"That's what an expense account is for. I know you have a problem with being paid for your services, but you shouldn't be carrying soggy tuna fish sandwiches when you're working for Sandy. Lunch is definitely a necessary perk."

I didn't argue. What I've learned since leaving St. Stephen's is that it's a lot harder to spend someone else's money than my own, and spending almost anything on non-essentials is hardest of all.

Jack left first to get to the Sixty-fifth by ten A.M. I left a little while later to get to the college well before my class began. Just before I scooted out, Mel called and asked if I wanted to meet her for lunch. I made a quick decision. Having missed a meal yesterday, I could afford a nicer lunch today and I looked forward to sharing it with Mel. She told me where to meet her and I hung up and ran.

I was brought up in the suburbs, not far from where I live now, so I have had no experience of living in New York. For me it was always a special place, the place where Daddy worked, where you went for parades and a trip to Radio City or the zoo, a place for a good time. I've been to New York many more times in the last year and a half than in the first thirty years of my life altogether, and although my opinion of the city has changed—as the city has—it's still a place that holds fascinations for me.

Greenwich Village is the area roughly around Washington Square, mostly to the west of it, although it has crept east. There are streets there with apartments so expensive, I couldn't imagine being able to afford to live in them, but there are also others in older buildings, farther from the center of the Village, that become manageable if you have a decent income or a roommate or two. The four-story building that bore the address Sandy Gordon had given me

had the age, charm, and slightly decrepit look that might fill
the bill.

I have visited many apartment houses in my amateur investigations and spoken to several superintendents, but this
time I was in for a surprise. The woman in apartment 1A
who answered my ring on Wednesday morning was the
owner.

"I've owned it seventeen years," she informed me after
I introduced myself, "and I pretty much remember everyone who ever lived here."

"I'm a friend of Sandy Gordon, who married Natalie
Miller about two years ago," I said.

"I remember Natalie well. Good tenant, paid her rent on
time. I think I saw him a couple of times, too. What happened?"

I told her.

She frowned as she listened. "Didn't someone come by
last year about that? A detective or something?"

"Very likely. Sandy hired him when the police had no
leads to Natalie's disappearance."

"And he didn't find her?"

"I'm afraid not."

"So you're looking now?"

"I'm trying. What can you tell me about her?"

"Just what I already said. Paid her rent on time, didn't
have any secret pets, left the apartment in pretty good
shape. Good tenant."

"When she moved in, did you get any references?"

"You mean like from friends?"

"Possibly."

"Friends say anything you want about them. Usually the
tenant types up the letter and the friend signs it. I use my
intuition and the bank."

"What did the bank tell you?"

"How much money she had. She gave me a check for
the first month and a month's security. The checks cleared.

And she gave me the name of the company she was working for. Want it?"

"Yes, please." There was just a chance she had lived here before she got the job with H and J.

"Come on in."

I had been standing in the foyer of the building. Now I followed her into her large living room. In the adjoining dining room, a file cabinet stood next to a desk. The woman, whose name I didn't know, pulled out a drawer and went straight to a folder about halfway through.

"Hopkins and Jewell," she called. "An ad agency. A Mrs. Wormholtz confirmed that Miss Miller was working for them."

"Anything else? Any previous address?"

"Sorry. She said she was new in town."

"Really?"

"That's why the bank account was new, too."

"Do you have any address for her? Where her family lives maybe?"

"I don't do that," the woman said, returning to the living room. "I did the first couple of years I owned the place. Called their mommies when they had crises, sat next to them when they threatened to end it all, that kind of thing. It got to be too much. I'm not their parents or their big sister or their loving aunt. I'm a landlord. If they need help, I dial nine-one-one. That's the beginning and the end of my responsibility."

"Do you remember Natalie having any crises?"

"Not really."

"Is anyone living here now who lived here when Natalie did?"

"As a matter of fact, yes." She thought for a moment. "I've got an old lady who's been here forever—I inherited her—and you could talk to her if you want. I don't think the detective talked to her."

"Why is that?"

"She usually takes a winter vacation and she was gone when he got here. Maybe he talked to someone else in the building, I don't know. But she's a good one. She lives on the top floor, right across from where Natalie lived. I'm sure they knew each other."

"May I have her name?"

"Mabel Bernstein. She's about eighty. I don't know how she does the stairs, but I guess she's just bound and determined not to leave this place alive."

I had a certain admiration for that. "Thank you very much."

"Go on up. She's probably packing now. She's leaving for her trip in a day or two."

The stairs were wide but sagging a little, the banisters a fine old wood, albeit scarred. Someone would buy this building one day and spend a small fortune to put it in shape, and then the rents would go sky-high. I found Mabel Bernstein's apartment to the left of the stairs and rang her bell.

"Who's there?" The voice sounded a challenge.

"Christine Bennett. The landlady sent me up."

The door was flung open. "No such thing." She was a little shorter than I, pure white hair, wearing a black skirt, white blouse, gray cardigan that could have been cashmere, and stockings and slippers. "No landlady in this place. She's a landlord. You can't know her very well."

"I just met her ten minutes ago, Ms. Bernstein. She said you would remember Natalie Miller."

"Mrs. Bernstein," she corrected me. "I'm not a miz and I'm not a miss. I remember Natalie very well. She lived over there." Pointing. "Are you coming in?"

"Yes, ma'am," I said, reverting to an earlier period of my life. I followed her into a large living room, past a bedroom with suitcases open on a large bed.

"I have nothing to offer you; the fridge is empty."

"Thank you. I'd just like to talk to you about Natalie.

Are you aware that she disappeared a little over a year ago?"

"I heard someone was here asking questions last year when I was in South America. I'm sorry to hear about Natalie. She seemed a nice person. Nice fiancé, too. I met him."

"Did she ever tell you where she was from? We're having a lot of trouble locating her family."

"There isn't any family. She said they'd died years ago. I was glad she met someone nice. There's nothing like family."

"Did she ever tell you where she lived before she moved here?"

"If she did, I don't remember."

"You said you met her fiancé. Did you ever meet any of the men she went out with before she met him?"

"I saw them. I can't say I met them."

"Did she ever talk about them?"

"Just to say, 'We're going to dinner Friday,' that kind of thing."

"No names?"

She looked around the room. It was a beautiful room with a fireplace and a mantel covered with framed pictures, candlesticks, magnificent old glass vases. She was a woman of taste and some means, even if—or perhaps because—she lived in an apartment whose rent was more typical of the sixties than the nineties. "Sandy is the one I remember best."

"That's the man she married."

"You think some old boyfriend did something to her?"

"I don't know. I just know we can't seem to trace her further back in time than five years ago, and this is the only address I have for her before she married."

"Susan," she blurted out. "Susan Diggins. They were friends."

"Yes, I've spoken to Susan."

"And she doesn't know anything?" She seemed shocked.

"They met at the agency that was Natalie's last job."

"Well, someone has to know where she's from."

"I'll keep looking," I said.

"There were men. I saw them. My opinion is, they weren't suitable."

"By which you mean—?"

"They were already spoken for. Or didn't amount to much."

"When are you leaving for your vacation?"

"Tomorrow." She looked at her watch. "I've still got a lot of packing to do."

I wrote my name and phone number on a scrap of paper. "If any of those names come back to you, would you call me collect?"

"From South America?"

"I want to find Natalie. Believe it or not, you're the last person on my list to talk to."

"And I haven't given you very much, have I?"

"You've been very helpful, Mrs. Bernstein. But if you think of anything else, I want to hear it as soon as possible."

"I'll do my best."

On my way out I talked briefly to the only other person at home in the building, a single woman with a bad cold. She remembered Natalie but knew nothing about her, had never said more than a greeting to her and added nothing to what I already knew. I thanked the nameless landlord when I got down to the first floor and then found myself out in the cold both literally and figuratively, asking myself what to do next and having no answer. I had checked out Natalie's last known address, last job, and last husband. I walked to where Greenwich Avenue ended at Sixth Avenue and located a phone. There I called Sandy Gordon.

"What've you got?" he asked with too eager anticipation.

"Unfortunately nothing. I've just been to the Greenwich Avenue address and I talked to an old woman that the detective missed because she was away last year."

"That's terrific," he said excitedly, and I regretted my phrasing.

"But she had nothing to add, Sandy. She didn't remember any of the people Natalie had known when she moved in except Susan Diggins, and I've seen her already. I gave her my phone number and told her to call collect from South America if she thinks of anything. I hope you don't mind."

"Of course not. Listen, where are you now?"

"On Sixth Avenue just south of Greenwich."

"Suppose I pick you up and take you to the house. I have a clear calendar today. When you're finished, I'll drive you home or hire a car for you."

"That's fine. Jack's in law school tonight, so I have no dinner to cook."

"Give me a quarter hour. Is there somewhere you can sit and have a cup of coffee?"

I was touched by his consideration. "I'm fine, Sandy. Just tell me where to stand."

"There's a bookstore on the southeast corner of Sixth Avenue and Eighth Street."

"I see it."

"I'll pick you up right there."

Fifteen minutes later, almost to the minute, he stopped at the curb and opened the car door for me.

14

Sandy drove an expensive German car that looked freshly washed, with fragrant leather seats and a dashboard that would have driven me crazy with its complexity. He kept up a pleasant banter as we drove through a tunnel and then along a highway to his New Jersey home. I found him very likable, and if I had any lingering suspicions that he himself might have been responsible for Natalie's disappearance, they were all but gone when he turned in to the driveway of a handsome new house whose garage door opened at the touch of a button.

We walked into a huge family room with a stone fireplace that took my breath away, and from there into a kitchen that his niece Melanie would probably sell her soul for. The counter was marble, the floor tile, the stove had six burners and a name I had never heard of, and the refrigerator looked large enough to store a couple of bodies in. Not that I thought it had ever been used for that purpose.

We had stopped along the way and picked up lunch, which we now sat and ate at the butcher block table in the large eating area just beyond the kitchen. When we were finished, Sandy dumped the leavings in the garbage and led me upstairs to the master bedroom.

It was quite a room, massive with wall-to-wall carpeting in a pale peach, and draperies and bedspread in precisely the same shade. The furniture was imposing and needed a bedroom of that size not to appear too large for its space.

The effect was breathtaking. I don't read many magazines and haven't been in many bedrooms in my life, so perhaps I was more taken than the Gordons' neighbors would have been, but the room was really impressive.

"That's Natalie's dresser. I've gone through it myself and found nothing, and I've removed only her more expensive jewelry and put it away for safekeeping. It was all things I had given her. You're welcome to go through it, and while you're here, if you want to, go through mine, too. I had no idea you were coming today, so I haven't prepared for this visit."

I felt embarrassed, but I knew I had to do it. "Let me ask you a couple of questions first. I had occasion the other day to go through some old cartons that come from my mother and have been in my basement for many years. Maybe my family is just unusually attached to mementos, but it occurred to me that Natalie must have brought things with her when you married."

"Very little. Mostly clothes, a handful of books—I think you saw them in the carton of stuff I dropped off at your house—and that's about it. You found those keys; I didn't even know they were there."

"Did you find any old handbags?"

"They're right here." He went to a double-doored closet that opened into a small room with floor-to-ceiling clothes, his and hers, expertly hung, shelved, and folded, and came out with several bags of different sizes, shapes, colors, and uses. "This is the one she always carried to work," he said, handing me a large, black leather shoulder bag. "She replaced it after we were married and she was carrying the new one when she disappeared."

"I'll start with this one."

"I'm going to leave you alone here, Chris. I'll be downstairs reading the paper. Take your time; I'm not in any hurry."

And with that he left the room, closing the door behind him.

I felt awkward sitting on the beautiful bed, so I pulled out the lovely silk-covered chair in front of Natalie's dressing table and sat on that. The bag, which was heavy even without the usual female paraphernalia, turned out to be as empty as one on a store counter, except that it didn't have any tissue paper stuffed in it to keep it in shape. When Natalie had switched to a new everyday bag, she had removed every item from the old one with the exception of a small mirror, a satin change purse that had nothing in it, and a worn emery board so deep in the folds of the zipper pocket that she could easily have missed it when cleaning out the bag. Natalie was obviously so compulsive about neatness that she left nothing behind when she abandoned one purse for another or she was just one of those people who kept only necessities in her purse, and everything needed to be moved. The new bag obviously provided her with the change purse and mirror she needed.

I set it aside and went through the others, a black suede handbag that contained clean tissues, several single dollar bills, probably handy for tipping, a rather elegant hand mirror that magnified the reflection, and nothing else; a gaily colored summer bag of woven straw that contained roughly what the black suede bag did; a handsome and clearly expensive black leather handbag with an Italian name inside and little else; and a small black bag of lizard and the softest leather I had ever touched, hung on a gold chain, and holding nothing but some tissues and a table assignment for Bill and Jenny's wedding. That was it.

Since I was sitting at the dressing table, I went through that next but found nothing of use to me. The enormous dresser was filled with the expected fine lingerie and sweaters, and again, no papers. I finished there and went to the closet. It was clearly divided into his and hers. Sure enough, half a dozen cruise outfits hung on the rack, all with their price tags. Natalie had left behind a wardrobe worth a fortune.

The bathroom, which was large and elegant, had a sunken tub with a Jacuzzi at one end, something I have yet to experience. A closet held sheets and bedding, dusting powder, skin lotions, and shaving necessities. A few prescription drugs had been issued from a local pharmacy.

Back in the bedroom I went through Sandy's chest, feeling like a voyeur. He had a passport in the top drawer, an old one issued several years ago, but there was none for Natalie. He had other papers that I merely glanced at before looking quickly through his shirts, socks, and underwear.

I was about to leave the bedroom when I noticed the night tables had drawers. I went over to one and opened it. Inside was a woman's novel with a bookmark about halfway through. I took it out and underneath found a diaphragm and a tube. To satisfy myself that she hadn't run off with a boyfriend, I flicked the plastic container open, saw the round object inside, and closed it.

There were a few magazines in the drawer and I flipped the pages, but nothing fell out. Then I turned my attention to Sandy's drawer. He, too, had books and magazines, some cough drops, a preparation for athlete's foot, and a couple of tubes of medication. I closed the drawer and went downstairs.

"Done?" Sandy stood as I entered the family room.

"I've gone over everything. I don't have a clue as to where Natalie comes from or what's happened to her."

Spread out in front of him was a stamp collection. He had been looking at something with a magnifier when I walked in. Now he put it down carefully.

"What else can I do for you? There must be something."

"A couple of things. Did Natalie go to a hairdresser?"

"Every week."

"Do you have the name?"

He thought a moment. "Sometimes she wrote a check. I'll look through my canceled checks. I'm sure I'll find it."

"Good. I saw your passport in your drawer, but I didn't see one for Natalie."

"As far as I know, she didn't have one."

"You were making a trip to an island that winter. Didn't she need a passport to get there?"

"We were going to St. John. It's an American possession. All you need is ID like a driver's license."

"Whose idea was it to go to St. John?"

"I think we decided together. It sounded like the kind of place we'd enjoy."

"Did she ever talk about the people at Hopkins and Jewell?"

"Sure. She liked them. They hired her early on and she had a kind of proprietary interest in the place. And they appreciated her. She got regular increases, they gave her special assignments, had her train new people."

"What did she think of Arlene Hopkins?"

He smiled. "I think Natalie thought she was a bright, arrogant woman who was tough to work for."

"Did Natalie work for her?"

"Not directly, but she worked for several people when she was needed."

"What about Eleanor Wormholtz?"

"Oh, Wormy. I'd say a love-hate relationship. Natalie respected her a great deal. Wormy wasn't a please-and-thank-you kind of person. She'd drop some work on Natalie's desk and say she needed it by five, and when Natalie gave it back at four o'clock, Wormy'd look at it and nod."

"What about Martin Jewell?"

"She said sometimes she thought of him like a brother. He was patient and understanding. If someone had a problem, they'd take it to him rather than Hopkins. He was the guy with the soft heart."

It certainly tallied with the way I had thought of him. "Steve Carlson?"

"I'm not sure I ever heard the name. There were a lot of names. This one said this, that one said that. They didn't stay with me. Of all of them, the only one I ever met was Susan."

"Can I have the name and address of the beauty parlor?"

"I'll be right down."

He left me and I went over to the table with the stamp collection. Next to the loose stamps he had been looking at was a shoebox of stamps torn off envelopes and occasionally whole envelopes. Near that were individual stamps and blocks of four in transparent envelopes. In a pile were several white envelopes addressed to Sandy, each with a different stamp on it. Every envelope was enclosed in transparent paper. Without touching, I looked at what was visible. I had not seen a stamp collection since I was a child, but I recalled that when Aunt Meg had written to me at St. Stephen's, she had always used commemorative stamps, and I wondered whether it was her interest or Uncle Will's that had led her to do so. I decided to start asking for them myself at the post office. I didn't write many letters, but unusual stamps would give my envelopes a slight distinction.

"Like my collection?"

I was surprised to see him back so soon. "It's beautiful. It must take a lot of your time."

"It's time I enjoy spending. My daughter enjoys it, too. I started both my kids off when they were young, but my son had no interest at all. I've got your name. It's called Hair Today and it's about a mile from here. Want to drop in on them?"

"Definitely."

"I'll get your coat."

"Yes, she's here and I think she's got a few minutes. Want to talk to her?"

"Yes, please." The receptionist disappeared around a corner as I waited. Sandy had come in with me and introduced himself, asking if the staff would cooperate. Then he'd gone out to the car after telling me to take my time.

The receptionist came back with a thin woman dressed in black tights and a red tunic. "Sharon, this is Christine Bennett. It's about Natalie Gordon."

"Oh, hi. Are you her sister?"

"I'm a friend of the family. Can we sit and talk?"

"Sure thing." She led the way to a group of chairs and asked if I wanted coffee. I said no and we sat away from two women waiting for their appointments.

"Do you know anything?" Sharon asked, her voice low and slow.

"No, not yet, that's why I'm here. I'm trying to help her husband find her. We thought you might have some information. How often did she come in?"

"Every Friday morning. Sometimes on Saturday if they were going somewhere important."

"What did she have done?"

"A blow-dry, a cut once a month, Diane did her nails every week."

"Was that it?"

"Well, a touch-up every once in a while."

"She colored her hair?"

"Oh yeah." She said it as though I really should have known without asking.

"What color was her natural hair?"

"Well, she was getting some gray, you know, and the natural brown was like losing its luster, you know what I mean?"

"Yes," I said, wondering for the first time in my life if my hair was losing something it had always had. "Was there a lot of gray?"

"There was quite a bit. Not like an old woman, but yeah,

it was happening to her. Some people just get gray prematurely."

"Can you show me what the color of her natural hair was? I mean the brown."

"Sure thing. Come with me." She got up and I followed her to a place on the wall where there were more hair colors than I'd ever seen in my life. Sharon ran her hand across a stretch of brown hair samples and stopped at one. "Kinda like this, but not as bright."

"Could you give me something like that to take with me?"

"I've got some in the back."

"And what about the color you dyed her hair?"

"That's this one. Glowing Auburn. It's nice, doesn't look too red. It's very natural. You want this one, too?"

"If I could."

"I'll be right back."

It was a long drive back to Oakwood, and we talked intermittently.

"Did you know Natalie dyed her hair?" I asked after a while.

"All women dye their hair. My first wife tried every shade of blond in the book and finally decided on the worst of them. She thought it made her look young; I thought it made her look old. I never asked Natalie whether she used color. Her hair looked very natural, and I suspect it was the color she was born with. I've known a lot of people who had red hair as kids, and I watched it turn brown as they got older."

What he said had merit and I had to agree both with him and with Natalie's hairdresser, that her hair looked very natural, at least from the pictures I had seen.

I didn't ask anything else. As we turned in to Pine Brook Road I said, "I don't know where I'm going from here, Sandy. I've given my name and phone number to a lot of people out there, but if I don't hear from them with new information, I'm really at a loss."

"Something will happen. You're doing all the right things. And I'm happy with your work. You'll know what to do. You've got the right instincts."

He turned up the driveway and we said good-bye. I had no idea my luck was about to change.

15

Over the next day there was a kind of explosion of information, just about all of it unexpected. It started as I put my things down in the house and went to check the answering machine. I have to say I feel uncomfortable having an answering machine in my home, but it came with my husband and I think of it as his, although messages are often left on it for me, as was the case today. I saw the blinking light and pressed the PLAY button.

"This message is for Miss Christine Bennett," a slow, careful elderly female voice said. "My name is Mabel Bernstein, B-E-R-N-S-T-E-I-N, and I spoke with Miss Bennett this morning. I have some information for her, but she'll have to call me back today because I won't be available tomorrow." She recited her number, added, "Please give her the message," and hung up.

The confusion was caused by Jack's security-conscious temperament. He refuses to identify us by name and has a rather grim-sounding order to leave a message at the tone. I dialed Mrs. Bernstein's number as fast as I could.

"Oh, Miss Bennett," she said happily, "I wasn't sure I'd reached the right number."

"That was my husband's voice. Tell me what your information is."

"I just remembered the name of the moving company Natalie used. They're Annie's Angels and they move people all over the Village."

117

"Annie? A woman's name?"

"We're a pretty independent lot down here. Anyone can do anything. And does."

"That's really terrific, Mrs. Bernstein."

"Well, I hope it gives you something to work on. You said I was the end of the line. At least now someone else is."

"I'm sure this is going to help. Thank you very much and have a wonderful vacation."

Before I got off the phone, she had given me Annie's Angels' phone number. I called immediately and got an answering machine. I supposed Annie was out doing her thing.

"He let us out early," Jack said, walking in half an hour before I expected him.

"Does he take a cut in pay for that?"

"He gets a round of applause."

"Coffee?"

"You bet." He followed me into the kitchen and opened the refrigerator, eventually taking out an apple. "How was your trip to the Village?"

"Profitable, but not until late this afternoon. And I got to see Sandy Gordon's house in New Jersey."

"Sounds like a busy day."

I told him.

"I'm hearing a few interesting inconsistencies," Jack said as I finished. He had taken a sheet of plain white paper and folded it in quarters as he does to take notes. Along the shorter fold he noted a few things as I spoke. "The landlady, or landlord as she prefers to be called, said Natalie was new in town, but Mrs. B. on the fourth floor, who knew Natalie a hell of a lot better than the landlord, says she used a local mover to move her stuff. Doesn't sound like it came from Indiana."

"Right. So she'd been living in New York before she

moved to Greenwich Avenue. And Wormy said she had references, one of which she checked. So Natalie had held at least two jobs in New York before coming to H and J."

"So we've got a lady who tailors her story to suit her purposes."

"But why?"

"Maybe she stiffed a landlord in New York, you know, moved out without paying the last month's rent or left the apartment in such a mess, she would have owed a lot of money."

"She didn't do that on Greenwich Avenue."

"She had a husband by then and she wanted him to think she was the greatest."

"That's possible." I looked over my own notes to see if I'd left anything out. "Oh yes. They were planning a vacation and Natalie had bought a lot of clothes for it, which she never wore. They all still had price tags hanging from them. Sandy has a passport. It's a few years old and I didn't look inside to see where he'd gone with it. But Natalie doesn't have one. They were going to St. John, which is an American possession, so she didn't need one."

"Her idea or his?"

"I asked him. He said they'd made the decision together. Sounds reasonable." I poured the coffee and put out some cookies.

"Can I say something?"

"When did you ever have to ask?"

He gave me the little smile that hinted something was coming. "Suppose you're talking to somebody and you mention you were married last summer and the person asks where. You say St. Stephen's Convent upstate and this woman says, 'What an interesting place to get married. Whose idea was that?' And you say, 'My husband and I picked it because I spent fifteen years there as a nun.' "

"Is that wrong?" I said, getting an odd feeling.

"Not wrong at all, just slanted. If I'd married any other

woman in the United States, would I have gotten married at St. Stephen's?"

"Well no, but—"

"But I married you, so I did. Do you remember when we first talked about it?"

I did. "You said your mother wouldn't be very happy about it."

"But we made the decision together and we did it. And I'm glad we did," he added, reaching across the table and touching my face. "You get my point? I would never say to anyone that we got married at St. Stephen's because my wife insisted. And if Natalie said to Sandy, 'Wouldn't it be nice to go to St. John?' the chances are he'd think it's a pretty nice idea and he'd tell you they made the decision together."

I did get the point. And Jack was right. Sandy always put the best face on everything that had to do with Natalie. It meant he wasn't the best source of information, although for many things he was my only source. "So it's possible she didn't want to get a passport. The reason is probably that she's older than Sandy thinks."

"Not unusual. Many women lie about their age."

"Her hairdresser said she had quite a bit of gray."

"Her hairdresser. That's good. You're a good investigator, Chris. Not that I didn't think so before."

"Her friend Susan is thirty-six and said Natalie claimed to be a few years younger, but Susan thought Natalie was Susan's age from things she had said."

"Sounds like she's a perceptive witness."

"I think she is. I may get back to her and ask her a few more questions. I wonder if Natalie was married, maybe even had children, and left them to start a new life."

"Sounds like a possibility."

"Maybe her former husband came to New York with the kids for the Thanksgiving Day parade and saw her there. That could really explain her disappearance." I could feel excitement building as the image took shape. "She couldn't run away from them because of the crowd, and he might follow her and see Sandy. So she goes along with him, knowing she's been found out and the new good life is over."

"I think that's an idea to work on," Jack said. "That the end of the cookies?"

"I'll get more tomorrow." That seemed to satisfy him and we went up to bed.

It wasn't even eight-fifteen when the phone rang the next morning. At the other end was Arnold Gold, already in his office preparing for a nine A.M. date in court.

"Got something for you," he said. "You awake enough for a hot piece of news?"

"Up and running."

"I was listening to my favorite music station as usual when I got into the office this morning. They have a report on the advertising world just after the eight-o'clock news, not anything that gets my blood going, but I heard a familiar name mentioned. Hopkins and Jewell. Isn't that where you said your missing woman worked?"

"Yes. What's the news?"

"They're breaking up."

"They're what?" I couldn't believe I'd heard right.

"Going their separate ways. Even the guy who broke the news on the radio seemed surprised. There hadn't been any rumors, the company'd been doing very well, only got together five years ago, et cetera, et cetera."

"I'm shocked. I don't know what to say."

"You ask them anything embarrassing?"

"Not that embarrassing. Some stuff is missing from Natalie's file. I asked if Hopkins could have taken it, but I don't really have a motive for her to have done so. Or at least not a strong one."

"Well, the advertising man said they would divvy up

their assets, work out some deal on the jobs they're working on, and split up."

"Thanks for keeping your ears open."

"I'd guess this'll be in today's *Times*. Back in the financial section if you read that far."

"Not usually. My quote assets unquote are in the same safe bonds my aunt bought."

"Probably just as well. Gotta tend to my law practice, Chrissie. Let me know what happens."

"I will." I hung up and reported to Jack, who was finishing up breakfast.

"I can't see what this has to do with your asking questions about a woman who worked for them a few years ago, even one who was in at the beginning."

"I can't either, but Arlene Hopkins really came across as trying to limit my access."

"Could be for ten other reasons."

"Could be. Maybe I'll give Wormy a call later on."

"Don't forget your Greenwich Village mover. I think that's your best bet at this point."

"Right." I looked at my watch. When the dishes were done, that would be my first call.

"Annie's Angels," a very sweet female voice answered.

"Good morning. My name is Christine Bennett and I have a question about someone you moved about five years ago. Her name was Natalie Miller and she moved to Greenwich Avenue."

"What do you need to know?"

"The address she moved from."

"I'm not sure I have the right to give that out. I'll really have to ask Annie. Can you tell me what this is all about?"

"She disappeared over a year ago and we're trying to trace her."

"What do you mean 'disappeared'?"

"She may have been kidnapped."

"This sounds a little crazy."

I couldn't dispute her judgment. "When can I reach Annie?"

"She usually comes in around nine. You want to call us back?"

"Yes."

"I'll tell her what it's all about when she comes in."

Since looking at Sandy's stamp collection, a few new ideas had started forming in my mind. When Jack and I were married, Jack asked his local post office in Brooklyn to forward his mail to his new address, our house in Oakwood. It was a natural thing to do. Old bills had to be paid, magazines had to be sent on, friends who had only your last address would want their mail to find its way to your new address. And there was something else that was a very long shot, but when you've got very little, you try anything. I dialed Sandy's number at work a little before nine—Jack had just set out for Brooklyn—and sure enough, he was there.

"Two things, Sandy," I said. "When you married, did Natalie have mail forwarded from the Greenwich Avenue address?"

"She didn't. She said she was tired of all the junk mail she got and this was a perfect time to cut it off. Her friends knew where she was going and she didn't care about anyone else. She paid the Con Ed bill, settled everything with her landlord, and didn't leave a forwarding address. I did, of course, and all my junk mail followed me. I don't think I ever saw a piece of mail with her maiden name on it."

"Second question. I noticed while you were upstairs yesterday that you had a lot of stamps still stuck to envelopes."

"That's right. Sometimes I save the whole envelope, sometimes just the stamp. I soak the stamps off, dry them, and put them in special albums."

"So you look over all the mail that comes into the house."

"Always. All collectors do. Nowadays a lot of mail is marked by a machine. It's mostly personal letters that have stamps."

"Did Natalie give you stamps off her envelopes?"

"All the time. She loved my collection. I don't think she'd ever seen a stamp collection before, and mine is pretty extensive. I showed her how to tear off the right part of the envelope, and every so often she'd give me a bunch. In fact, I remember when we were first married, she— Chris, you're a genius."

"What is it?"

"She gave me an old stamp from an envelope that had been mailed a long time before. She started to tear it wrong and I stopped her and showed her what I wanted, including the postmark."

"Sandy, did you see how it was addressed? I know it was a couple of years ago, but do you remember anything at all about that envelope?"

"It was handwritten. That's all I caught. She tore off the stamp, with the postmark, and gave it to me. It'll take me some time, but I can find it for you. I'm sure that's in a box that I haven't worked on yet."

"OK. That's your assignment. Maybe we'll find somebody somewhere who knows Natalie Miller."

"You'll hear from me."

That gave me a lift. If it came from someplace in Indiana, we could take out ads in local newspapers. I wondered whether Miller was her maiden name or the name of someone she had married. Sandy's explanation of how she had not left a forwarding address certainly pointed to a woman trying to lose her past.

At a few minutes after nine I called Annie's Angels again, and this time Annie herself was there. She asked why I wanted the information on Natalie and I told her the truth.

"I remember her," Annie said, not giving anything away. "I went to her old apartment to give her an estimate."

"Do you have that address?" I crossed the fingers of my free hand.

"I do, but I don't know who you are and I'm kind of reluctant to give it out."

"I'll be glad to come down to your office. I can be there before noon."

"What the hell, it's five years." She gave me an address on the east side over near Gramercy Park.

"You said you remembered her. I wonder if I could ask you a couple of questions." I went on, not giving her a chance to turn me down. "Did she have a roommate?"

"She's the only one I talked to and the only one I saw. She signed the contract and she paid for the move."

"How did she pay?"

"In cash. That's not unusual. We don't take checks unless they're certified. In this business, it's easy to get stiffed."

"Was the apartment pretty much a one-person residence or did it look like there might have been a family or another person living there?"

"It had one bedroom, but there were two beds in it. We only agreed to move one of them. She said she was selling the other one."

"Do you remember anything about the furniture? Did it look like the kind of stuff you pick up at the Salvation Army or was it bought new?"

"I'd have to say a mixture. People don't usually spend the money to move old furniture that they can replace. It just doesn't pay. She had an old Formica kitchen table that she didn't move either, and a couple of chairs. All she moved from the kitchen was a box of dishes and some pots and pans. The living room furniture went. I have that down here."

"Thanks very much, Annie."

"This gal's really missing?"

"Over a year. Since Thanksgiving of the year before."

"I hope you find her. I'll ask the guys if they remember anything."

"I'd appreciate it."

So there might have been a roommate. It was like pulling teeth, but at least I was starting to get somewhere. And the picture was not all that promising for Sandy. It certainly appeared as though Natalie had tried mightily to cover her tracks. Only Susan Hartswell, of all the people I had spoken to, knew where she had gone when she got married. I picked up the phone and dialed her number. She answered quickly.

"Susan? This is Chris Bennett."

"Oh, hi. Have you found Natalie?"

"No, I've just picked up a few crumbs of information. I've got an address for where she lived before she moved to Greenwich Avenue."

"That's great." She sounded genuinely happy. "Maybe someone there will remember her."

"I hope so. I'm going to visit the building today. I just heard some news that may interest you. Hopkins and Jewell are breaking up."

"You can't be serious."

"It was on the radio this morning, on the advertising news. They're splitting into two companies."

"I can't believe it. They're, you know . . ." Her voice trailed off.

"They're what?"

"Well—lovers. At least I thought they were."

"I see. Maybe the magic ended."

"I guess it would be tough to be partners if the other relationship came to an end."

"I would think so," I said.

"Keep me posted."

I promised I would.

16

Gramercy Park is one of those pleasant anomalies in Manhattan, a private park, fenced in and locked, with keys available to the residents of certain buildings in the area. Ads for apartments often include the fact of a key. I had never been in it, although I had walked alongside it on several occasions. It lies between East Twentieth and East Twenty-first Streets only a block or so west of the Police Academy. On this sunny Thursday morning two women sat on a bench moving their strollers idly back and forth to keep their youngsters content.

I found the address Annie had given me. It was a small apartment house about a block from the park, and I guessed there were no keys to the park for the tenants. A superintendent with an apartment on the first floor instead of in the basement opened the door at my ring. The person turned out to be a woman and she said she remembered Natalie Miller.

"Do you know how long she lived here?" I asked.

"Maybe one lease, like two years."

"Did she have any roommates?"

"Oh, honey, I couldn't tell you that. They all do now. There was a time you had some control over who lived in your building, but no more. The courts let them do anything. She's the only one who signed the lease."

"Do you remember another woman sharing the apartment?"

"It could be."

"A man?"

"Like I said—"

"Do you know if she moved out in a hurry?"

"Lemme check." She consulted a file in a cabinet in the room we were talking in. "She didn't skip out without paying if that's what you mean. We let her apply her security to the last month's rent because there wasn't any damage to the apartment and it says here she left in the middle of the month."

"Do you remember anything about her?"

"They come and go," she said. "When they're gone a while, I can't really tell you very much."

"Does anyone still live near her old apartment that lived there five years ago?"

"You got me. Not right near her, I don't think. We been renovating those apartments, getting them off rent control one by one. Hers was first, then one across the hall. Hold on." She went to a different file and turned some pages. "There's a couple down the hall you could talk to. They've been living there six, seven years, since they got married. There's two kids there now. They're dying to buy a house in the suburbs, but they can never afford one. I'll take you up."

They were on the third floor and I could hear the children before we rang the doorbell. The woman inside shouted something at them and then opened the door. She was only about my age and quite pretty, dressed in wool pants and a paisley blouse with a couple of gold chains. The super made a quick introduction and then left us.

"Come on in, I'm Dickie Foster," she said.

"Hi. Chris Bennett."

"My kids are driving me crazy, but they'll probably calm down now that there's company."

She was right. They were suddenly silent and wide-eyed, staring at me as though I were a visitor from a foreign planet. I smiled and said hello to them, and the younger one, a little girl, giggled and covered her face with her hands.

We went into the living room, which was set up like a day care center, a small, colorful wooden slide in one corner, toys everywhere, balls of all sizes. We walked through the children's area and sat near the windows, the only part of the room that still looked as though it catered to adults.

"What can I tell you?"

"I'm trying to find Natalie Miller. Do you remember her?"

"That's a long time ago, isn't it?"

"About five years."

"She lived down the other end of the hall, didn't she?"

"So I'm told."

"We used to say hello, sure."

"Anything else? Were you friendly? Sit and talk once in a while?"

"Not really. I was working when we moved in, and she was, too."

"Do you know where?"

She shook her head.

"Did she ever have a roommate?"

"Male or female?"

"Either."

"Some guy used to come out with her in the morning sometimes. We'd meet in the elevator. That was when we first moved in."

"How long ago is that?"

"We've been married seven years."

"Seven years ago," I said. "And then what?"

"Then he wasn't there anymore."

"Female roommates?"

"Toward the end someone was with her, I think. I don't know the name. I only saw her once or twice."

"Did Natalie say good-bye to you before she moved?"

"You know, I think she did. I think she said something about a job she was interested in. She'd answered an ad and they called her for an interview. She was pretty excited about it."

"She must have been even more excited when she got it."

"Maybe, but I don't remember anything about that. She just moved. I never saw her again."

The super had said she had moved in the middle of the month, so I assumed there hadn't been a lot of time for good-byes. And Dickie Foster certainly didn't speak of her as a friend. As usual, I wrote my name and phone number on a scrap of paper and gave it to her. "If you ever think of a roommate's name or if you remember Natalie ever telling you where she came from or where she was going to, I'd appreciate a call."

"You said you were trying to find her. What happened?"

"She went to the Thanksgiving Day parade with her husband the year before last and disappeared. No one's seen or heard of her since."

"How bizarre."

I stood. "So anything, anything at all."

"I'll rack my brain, I promise. It's nice she got married. What's he like?"

"A very nice divorced man who was crazy about her. Is," I corrected myself. "He wants to find her. Tell me, what's your estimate of how old Natalie was when you knew her?"

"Back then? Not old. Twenties, late twenties. Something like that. I'm terrible on ages." Which put her back at the age she claimed for herself.

I thanked Dickie and walked down the hall to the elevator, stopping in front of Natalie's apartment. It had been renovated, the super told me, but the door looked as old as Dickie Foster's. On a far-out chance, I took Natalie's key ring out of my bag and tried the first key in the lock. It turned easily. Feeling a little panicky, I relocked the door, got in the elevator, and rode downstairs.

"You picked the worst day of my life to call." Wormy sounded pretty down on the phone.

"I heard the news," I said from the pay phone I had found on a street corner near Gramercy Park. "Is there any connection between what's happening and my questions about Natalie Miller?"

"I can't talk to you about that. Let me get Marty on the line."

I waited, hoping I wouldn't become disconnected, but after a brief silence, he came on the line.

"Miss Bennett? This is Martin Jewell."

"Mr. Jewell, I wondered if we could talk for a minute."

"Are you somewhere close?"

"Not far."

"Meet me outside the building in ten minutes. We'll have lunch."

"I'll be there."

"I was nuts about her."

We were sitting in a very nice restaurant a couple of minutes walk from H and J, the kind of place I hadn't dressed for but no one seemed to care. We hadn't been given a table near the kitchen or anything approaching that, so I guessed that Jewell's presence was all that counted.

"Natalie," I said.

"Natalie. I'm telling you this not because I feel the need to confess but because I know you're having a hell of a time finding her. I know a couple of things no one else knows. I don't know if I can help, but I'll try."

"Thank you."

"I never saw her until the moment she walked into my office to be interviewed. I'd looked at her resumé—and I can't remember where she worked—and decided she was promising. She crossed the threshold and that was it. I have a wife and two kids and I've had something going with Arlene for a long time, at least it was going until recently. I needed an assistant because Wormy is my cousin and she didn't want to take orders from me. That's how she put it. She felt we'd all be better off if she kept her independence."

It's nice to hear similar stories from different people, and this one had the ring of truth. "Go on."

"What can I tell you? It just happened. We were around each other and something clicked. We began an affair."

"Did anyone know?"

"Arlene probably suspected. I didn't see her as much, so she had reason to ask questions. We were very discreet, believe me."

"Did Natalie want to marry you?"

"I'm the wrong guy to ask. I never know what women want. I wanted her body and I assumed she wanted mine."

"Where did you meet?"

"At her apartment sometimes."

"On Greenwich Avenue?"

"The same. Sometimes we'd stay late in the office and work. I had a couch in my old office."

"But the affair ended," I said.

"Long before she left. And it ended because I couldn't handle it anymore. I had a family and I had a partner who was more than a partner. It was too much. I told her we had to stop."

"But she stayed on in the company. That must have been very uncomfortable."

"I thought it would be worse if she left. I thought Arlene would really figure out for sure that something had been going on and now it was over. I kind of eased Natalie into other work so we didn't see as much of each other. I'll tell you something. It was a relief when she met Sandy. He was the right kind of guy for her."

"What do you mean?"

"He was available."

I was eating a delicious seafood salad and Martin Jewell was sipping a drink and eating a big green salad with diet dressing. "Did she ever talk about her family?"

"Very little, no specifics, no names."

"Did you ever go away together?"

"Once. We spent a weekend down at Cape May in New Jersey. We couldn't go to Long Island because everyone I know has a house out there."

"Who picked Cape May?"

"I did."

That had certainly been an unequivocal answer. "Did you ever go to the apartment she lived in before she moved to Greenwich Avenue?"

"Didn't know she had one. Wormy might have known. She sends out the checks. I have something else to tell you."

It sounded ominous and I put my fork down and drank some of the sparkling water he had insisted on ordering.

"I gave her a key to the office."

"I see." I opened my bag, felt around and found the key ring. "Is it one of these?"

"This one."

"What you're telling me—"

"What I'm saying is, I don't think Arlene took those papers out of Natalie's file. Wormy wouldn't do it and she had no cause to. I know I didn't. Arlene is pissed because she thinks you think she took the stuff in Natalie's personnel file. I think Natalie took them."

"Can you think of a reason why she would do that?"

"She was a very secretive kind of person. I never got the feeling she was hiding anything, just that there were things she'd rather not talk about. She didn't have a great childhood somewhere in the middle of this country. She was born into a family that didn't exist anymore. She lived for today. I never had the feeling she sent birthday cards to people the way my wife does."

"Why did you give her the key, Mr. Jewell?"

He looked a little uncomfortable at my formality. "We met at the office sometimes. We never left together. If I left first, she would wait half an hour and then go."

"Did you ever see Natalie after she married?"

"Not once. And I never saw her again intimately after the night we broke up."

"Did you ever meet Sandy?"

"Her husband?"

"Yes."

"Uh-uh."

"Do you think Natalie might have been married before she came to work for you?"

"Wouldn't surprise me. You think she was running away from someone?"

"Among other possibilities."

"There was something missing from her. I can't tell you what it was, but it almost scared me. Maybe you hit on it. Maybe there was an abusive husband in her life that she never wanted to see again."

"How old do you think she was?" I asked, tossing out my last question.

"Ageless," he said with a smile. "Like me. It's what we had most in common."

So there I was again with nowhere to go and a variation on my theme that sounded as plausible as my own idea. Somehow the notion of an abusive husband hadn't occurred to me, perhaps because I don't like to think about things like that, but it would certainly explain a lot of what I now knew. A woman who wants to cover her tracks because of fear of being found by someone who might hurt her is exactly the person who would remove papers with her home-town, high school, and last address on them. If Natalie had come to New York as a young single woman and married here, her husband—or ex-husband—might never have met anyone from her hometown. I had certainly heard enough horror stories of women being stalked by ex-husbands to be impressed with the seriousness of such a situation. My own version, of a wife deserting a family, was surely less flattering to Natalie. Martin Jewell's version, an abused wife, was far more sympathetic but potentially more deadly. An abusive man whom she had escaped from was far more likely to kill when and if he found her.

It gave me plenty to think about on the train ride home. And as I put things together, I found a deep well of sympathy for Natalie. I had never believed she had voluntarily left Sandy, and nothing I had heard or seen since our first conversation had changed my mind. She seemed a contented woman—of whatever age—who had achieved what she wanted, a good husband, a beautiful home, the chance, finally, to have a child. Her life before she met Sandy Gordon had been hit-or-miss at best, and perhaps deeply disturbing. I found that I accepted the possibility that she had stolen her own documents as true. Not only had Martin Jewell claimed to have given her a key to the office, he had identified the one possible key it might have been. She was a woman covering her tracks. What if her former lover-husband had found out where she was working and called H and J as though he were a prospective employer? Whether Natalie had any friends or relatives left in whatever place she came from, he might start snooping around to find her. She might not send birthday cards as Mrs. Jewell did, but she might send a Christmas card or two and someone might be able to furnish a lead.

But where did she come from? Where had she gone? And how was I going to find out?

17

I heard Jack's car pull up the driveway just as the phone rang, a late hour for anyone to be calling. It was Sandy Gordon in a state of great excitement.

"I've been at it all night and I found it," he said.

"The stamp?"

"The stamp and the piece of envelope it's attached to, including a postmark."

"Sandy, that's wonderful. Where did it come from?"

"Indiana. I told you she came from Indiana. The postmark says Connersville. I've already checked it out. It's a small city east of Indianapolis and not far from the Ohio border. Of course, she may not have lived right in that town. The letter may just have been posted there."

"I understand, but it's a good starting point. Is there anything else?"

"No, that's it. Will you go out there?" His excitement was so high, he sounded like a kid.

"Jack's just coming in the house. I'll talk to him about it and call you tomorrow."

"Am I glad you saw my stamp collection."

"So am I, Sandy. Have a good night."

"It's starting to sound very promising," Jack said when I'd finished my story. He was snacking on leftovers and we were sharing a pot of coffee and some cookies I'd bought before I got home this afternoon.

"Do I go out there?" I asked. "There must be a million Millers in the Midwest."

"I think it's too soon for that. Give me a couple of good shots of her and I'll fax them out to Connersville and maybe some towns in the area. Let's see if the name means anything or the picture means anything."

"She could have married a high school sweetheart," I said. "There's a chance his family might recognize her even if she has no family of her own left. Or people she went to high school with."

"Anything's possible. Just pick out a couple of good ones and remind me about her hair color."

"It was brown originally."

"What about her height and weight?"

"I'll show you some wedding pictures where she's standing next to Sandy. You're a better judge of that than I."

He figured her for about five six and 125 to 135 pounds. He wrote down her age as thirty-three to thirty-eight, spanning the range of estimates.

"You know that if anything turns up, I have to give my information to the detective who's holding the case."

"Sure," I said. "I'm not looking for an exclusive on this."

"How nice to work with an amateur," Jack said with a grin. "Sure you're not looking for a collar?"

"Just a woman. Hopefully alive."

"Don't get those hopes up too high."

It wasn't easy to follow his suggestion. He called the next day after he had faxed the picture to several police and county sheriffs' departments and to the Indiana and Ohio State Police. He also spoke to someone at each location and asked about Natalie Miller. As I had surmised, Miller was a fairly common name—one officer said there were columns of Millers in the phone book—and no one had a criminal file for a woman of that name. Nor was Natalie listed in a phone book, which didn't surprise me.

Jack got the name of a newspaper in the area from one police officer and called to see if I could place an ad, together with a picture. When he faxed the picture, the paper said it looked interesting but they'd rather have an original if he could overnight it. By that time Jack had had a number of copies made at a place in Brooklyn the police used, so we put together a few lines of copy and gave Sandy's business address and his home phone number for responses, and Jack arranged to have the ad run for three days, Sunday through Tuesday. Then I let Sandy know about it.

Late in the afternoon the phone rang and I heard Dickie Foster's voice and the kids giggling in the background.

"Is this Christine Bennett?"

"Yes, it is. Dickie?"

"Right. My husband reminded me of something. We talked about Natalie last night. He remembers meeting her in the elevator, too, and he also remembered that when she was with that guy, the one I told you about who stayed with her when we first moved in, she introduced him as her brother."

"Did she give a name?"

"My husband thinks it was Terry. I'm just not sure. And frankly, I'm not convinced he was her brother. She may just not have wanted us to know she was living with some guy."

"You mean she was embarrassed about it?"

"She may have been. Also she may have been worried about having someone stay with her that wasn't on the lease."

"Dickie, I can't thank you enough for calling. And thanks to your husband for his good memory. If anything else occurs to you, I'd like to hear about it."

"There is something else. Remember I told you the last

time I talked to Natalie was when she applied for a job? And then she went away and I never saw her again? I actually heard from her."

"How?"

"She must have taken a little vacation around the time she moved. She sent us a postcard."

"Do you remember where it came from?"

"No, but it could turn up. I'm a real pack rat, and things like postcards are hard for me to throw away. If I come across it, I'll call you."

"That would be great," I said. That was an understatement.

The weekend was quiet and Jack and I spent it together. We did some walking, took in a movie at the old movie theater that had recently been converted to four smaller ones, and brought home a pizza laden with everything you can imagine for a late dinner.

"So your ad gets published in Indiana tomorrow," Jack said, sprinkling hot pepper flakes on his first slice.

"I don't think Sandy's leaving the phone for a minute."

"If someone recognizes her, they'll call."

"What if it's twenty years since she left and her looks have changed so much, no one recognizes her?"

"I've got an idea on that, but let's give it a couple of days. Anything new on your father and the mystery woman?"

"Nothing. But I have a new thought. We lived in the house I grew up in for about ten years, and my mother was very friendly with one of the neighbors, a woman named Elsie Rivers. If Elsie's still there, she might be able to remember something—if my mother confided in her, which is iffy."

"Sounds like a good idea. She listed in the phone book?"

"There's a Rivers on the right street. It's funny, I haven't been back to the old house since my mother died. Aunt

Meg put it up for sale and took care of everything. Maybe I'm old enough to see it again."

"Want me to go along?"

"I'd love it."

"What's a Sunday for?"

Houses get smaller and trees get bigger. We had planted the dogwood in the front yard not long after we moved in, a small, wispy thing that produced lovely pink flowers in the spring and bright red berries in the fall, only not many of either. Now it had spread itself to shade most of the downstairs of my early home. Even leafless it had the grace and delicacy of a mature dogwood, and I felt my heart do funny things as I looked at it from the car.

Jack took my hand. "You OK?"

"I thought it was such a big house."

"You were such a little girl."

"I guess so."

"Want to ring the bell?"

"No." But I couldn't take my eyes off the house and the tree.

We sat in silence for another minute. Then Jack said, "How do I find Elsie Rivers?"

"Circle the block. She lived behind us, one or two houses down."

We drove slowly to the corner.

"No," the plump woman with big glasses said in amazement. "You're Francie's little girl? You're Kix Bennett?"

She wrapped her arms around me and I felt as though I had come home to my own, the prodigal daughter returned. A mite tearfully I introduced Jack and she pulled us inside to the warmth of her living room.

"Oh my Lord," she said, "if only Francie could have lived to see this. Sit down, kids, sit down. Let me just push away the paper. I read the Sunday paper all over the living room." She gathered up sections quickly and dropped them on the floor where they were out of the way.

We accepted her hospitality because we couldn't refuse. She made tea—I remembered her and my mother sitting over teacups in the afternoon—and found half a coffee cake that was restored to life with the heat of a toaster oven. Then we talked, Jack listening more raptly than I had anticipated. I told her everything that had happened since the death of my mother. She wept as she remembered moments of their friendship, my mother's illness, her own last moments with me. I didn't linger or dwell. When we were up to date she was smiling just as I remembered her.

"So you're a married woman now with your own home. Oh, Francie would have loved it. And Eddie, too. Never was a nicer man than your daddy, Kix."

I felt a little embarrassed. It wasn't going to be that easy, asking for secrets. "I was especially remembering him recently," I said. "Someone mentioned the Thanksgiving Day parade and I remembered how he used to take me."

"I'm not surprised. You were the apple of his eye. I'll bet your mom never went to those parades."

"She didn't."

"Too cold for her. She hated the cold weather. I think she had southern blood in her veins. She was always putting on a sweater when I was taking mine off."

"I remember," I said. "But my dad wasn't like that."

"Oh, he couldn't be. He was always out meeting clients. I remember he used to go through shoe leather like nobody else."

I felt comforted by hearing these little details of my parents' lives. As she spoke, I could see my mother checking the thermostat—never putting it higher because that would cost money—and then going for a sweater. And I remembered Daddy's shoes. I always wait till I get a hole in the second one to have them soled, he would say. How wonderful to hear their voices again, to see them as they were.

"Elsie, I'm going to ask you something a little odd, something you may know about. When my father took me to the parade, we used to meet someone there, a woman that I never saw anywhere else. She didn't work with Dad, but she may have lived near Central Park West in the Sixties where we watched the parade. Do you have any idea who she might have been?"

"Not the faintest. Why would I?"

"I thought maybe Mom talked to you about her."

A shadow of a frown formed on her amazingly smooth forehead. She had round apple cheeks and fewer wrinkles than women ten years younger than she. "I don't think I understand," she said.

"My father had one sister, my aunt Meg, who I lived with after Mom died. As far as I know, he never had any others. If he had some woman friend, maybe my mother knew her or mentioned her to you." I couldn't come out and make an overt suggestion of a breach of my father's fealty.

"Your father was as good as they come, Chris, as loyal and true as a husband and father could be. That woman was just someone taking her kids and herself to the parade. There's no more to it than that."

We stayed a little longer because she didn't want to let us go. Finally Jack took his detective's card out of his pocket, wrote my name and our home address and phone number on it, and gave it to her. She hugged us both and walked us outside the door, the cold apparently not affecting her. She stood there waving till we started up the car, then threw a kiss and went inside.

"Quite a gal," Jack said.

"I'd forgotten the sweaters and the shoe leather. They were always so careful, always saving for a future that never came."

"It became your future, and I think you're living the life they wanted for you."

"I think she knows something, Jack."

"That's why I gave her my card. If the spirit ever moves her and she feels she can't talk to you, she might call me at the station house."

"And you'll tell me whatever she says."

"Of course," he said easily. "What else?"

There was no message on the machine from Sandy and I decided not to call. I would hear from him when he was ready, or when he had something to tell me. The call came after we had finished dinner.

"Nothing, Chris," he said, sounding like the end of the world. "Not a single call."

"Give the ad the whole three days, Sandy. People may not want to call on a Sunday."

"This has just got to be the right place. Even if she didn't live there herself, the person who wrote to her knows her."

"I think we're going to find her," I said. I hadn't told him half the things I'd learned since Thursday, but I was very encouraged by the new information.

"I'll call you," he said, and hung up.

"Nothing?" Jack asked.

"Nothing. I think the time has come to make a visit to St. Stephen's."

18

Summer or winter, I never mind the drive to St. Stephen's Convent. There is always the rush of feeling when I see the roofs and spires in the distance. It was my home for fifteen wonderful years, and I left as a friend of the convent and a friend of every nun I had loved while I was there. The woman I knew best and whom I consider my closest friend to this day was Sister Joseph, now serving her first term as General Superior. While she is considerably older than I, she is distinctly of my generation, not of the one that preceded her. As an administrator she runs the convent the way a successful business should be run, and I wouldn't flinch at the thought of having her take over a large secular company and watch it grow, although that will never happen.

There is, of course, the other, more important side to her. When I was a member of the convent, Joseph was my spiritual director, and it was she who guided me during the difficult year of my decision to leave. It was also she who welcomed me as a bride last summer, and I've never had any doubts that she arranged the perfect weather that accompanied our beautiful wedding in St. Stephen's chapel.

As always, I started my visit with a walk around the convent grounds, which include the women's college I had taught in for many years. A bell rang as I approached the college campus, and a moment later students and brown-habited nuns poured out of the buildings, talking, laughing, enjoying their youth and their education. I watched them with my usual feelings of nostalgia, hoping to see a familiar face.

"Sister Edward?"

I turned. A tall, thin girl bundled in a blue down jacket stood beside me. "Janine?" I asked hesitantly, irritated that my memory was failing me.

"Yes. Janine O'Brien. How are you? It's been a long time, hasn't it?"

"A year and a half. You must be graduating this year."

"I am. I've applied to graduate school in a lot of places. I think I'll go on in English."

"That's wonderful."

"What are you doing now?"

"Unexpected things," I admitted. "I got married last summer and I work at a couple of part-time jobs."

"Married," she said, as though the news had stunned her.

"I met him after I left St. Stephen's. It was all pretty surprising." I looked at my watch. "I have an appointment with Sister Joseph. Are you walking toward the Mother House?"

"I've got to get back to the dorm."

"It's been wonderful seeing you. Good luck. And I'm Chris Bennett now. If you want a recommendation for graduate school, Sister Joseph will give you my address."

"Thank you." She seemed flustered. "I may just do that. 'Bye."

I watched her go, then turned and hurried off for my appointment.

"Whatever the reason, it's good to see you," Joseph said, giving me a hug.

I had run the gauntlet downstairs, saying hello to everyone I ran into. The long table in Joseph's office was set with the expected tea and cups, some cookies that had the look of a nun's hands-on loving care.

"From the villa," Joseph said. "No one will ever forget what you did for us at Christmas."

"Not enough, I'm afraid," I said with the touch of sadness that the memory of the past Christmas would always evoke in me. "The debt is all mine."

"There are no debts among friends," Joseph said with finality. "Sit down. I'm eager to hear about your case. You were chintzy with details on the phone, if I may say so."

I sketched the story, as I always did when I came to Joseph for help. She had her stack of unlined paper and pencils beside her, and as we sipped tea and munched on cookies she took notes, interrupting from time to time to ask questions.

In a very literal way, I laid my case on the table, showing her pictures of Natalie and finally putting the ring of keys down between us.

"And where did these come from?" she asked.

"From a carton Sandy brought over before I agreed to work on the case. There were some books of Natalie's, inscribed by men but none of them a Terry, some cosmetics she used, their wedding album and some loose pictures, quite a few because Sandy must have taken every opportunity to photograph her."

"So the carton was brought into the marriage, so to speak, by Natalie and added to by her husband."

"That's the way it looks to me. He claimed never to have seen the keys, so I guess they must have fallen out of an envelope of pictures."

"And which of the keys have you identified?"

"This small one opened the desk she sat at at Hopkins and Jewell. This one turned the front-door lock in the apartment she lived in five years ago. And this one Martin Jewell identified as opening the door of their old office."

She looked at the remaining keys, the ones that probably opened suitcases. "So they represent Natalie's old life.

When she left Hopkins and Jewell to get married, she started a new key ring."

"Which is probably in the purse she was carrying when she disappeared."

"Let me think about these keys for a moment. She couldn't return the door key to Hopkins and Jewell because no one except Mr. Jewell knew she had it."

"She could have returned it to him."

"True, but perhaps she didn't want to be alone with him or perhaps she'd even forgotten about the key. Presumably she hadn't used it for some time."

"If we accept his story, that's true."

"And she couldn't turn it in to this Wormy person because Wormy doesn't know Natalie's been given a key."

"Right."

"But she also kept the key to her desk before she left."

"It would seem so," I said. "Maybe that key is the oversight. I've begun to think she kept the key to the office in case she wanted to check out her file again."

"A bit of paranoia," Joseph said.

"If there was someone in her past whom she had reason to be afraid of, she didn't want her new address and name in their files. I know they sent her a W Two form after she disappeared."

Joseph made a note. "So they had to have her new name and address."

"Until January of last year. Maybe she was planning to sneak back one night and get rid of it after tax season."

"It's probably on a computer now, but from what you've said, she would have been knowledgeable enough to know the system and expunge any damaging information. Of course, we'll never know if she intended to." Joseph picked up the ring of keys. "It's this key that concerns me most." She held up the key to the door of the apartment near Gramercy Park. "It's marked Segal. That's the name of a lock that's used a lot in New York apartments, and if it has the name of the lock on it, it's one of the original keys that was issued with the lock."

"Are you sure about that?"

She pulled her own large ring of keys out and found one to show me. "I had this one made just a few days ago. It's a duplicate for a broom closet in the dormitory. The original is marked with the name of the lock, but this one isn't. This one is stamped Morgan Hardware, the hardware store in town. Just out of curiosity I asked the locksmith there about it when he was cutting it for me. He said duplicates don't have the name of the lock on them. They may have the name of the company that makes the blanks like Ilco, the International Lock Company, or they may be stamped by the hardware store or locksmith with their name, as mine is."

I looked at Natalie's key. "So this is an original key, probably the one the landlord gave her or the locksmith if she had the lock installed herself."

"My question is, how could she have gotten away with not turning in the key? If they're still using the same lock, they must have gotten a key back."

"Maybe a roommate had a duplicate, or the brother."

"Which means she returned the duplicate and kept the original. A little odd, don't you think? Well, perhaps it was more convenient to return the duplicate; it wasn't on her key ring. But I think it warrants a phone call, Chris."

I agreed and wrote it down. "There's a possible explanation for why she only returned one key," I said, thinking it over. "She didn't want the landlord to know she'd had overnight guests, male or female."

"Good thinking. If she returned two keys, there might be questions. Funny, though, that she returned the duplicate, not the original."

"No answer, Joseph. Not at this point anyway."

"Let's see where we are. We have a good-looking woman in her thirties who, like many women, uses cosmetics and hair color to enhance her looks and make her look younger, a woman who married the man of her dreams, lives in the house she has always wanted, and now is possibly pregnant with a child. Nothing unusual anywhere except that her life seems to start five to seven years ago and she is the best suspect for removing all evidence of her earlier life from her personnel record. Would she have removed those papers if she had married Martin Jewell?"

"She may have removed them quite early in her employment, early enough that her relationship with him was still going on."

"So it wasn't a question of whom she married—or was intimate with—it was a matter of keeping her past a secret from everyone."

"And one reason for doing that may have been in order to hide from one person who had the power to destroy everything she had built, perhaps even to kill her."

"She certainly did an effective job of it. The police haven't found her, a private detective failed, and although you've come closer than anyone else, no one has answered your ad in the Indiana paper. All of which means she's well hidden or dead, and if she's dead, her body has been well hidden." She looked down at her notes. "Tell me again what the neighbor, Dickie Foster, said."

"They moved in as newlyweds about seven years ago, so they lived there for two of the years Natalie was there. Early on they met her in the elevator with a man she introduced as her brother, possibly named Terry. They had a casual acquaintanceship, but when Natalie moved out, after very excitedly telling Dickie she was being interviewed for a great job, she dropped the Fosters a postcard from somewhere."

Joseph smiled. "And that somewhere may be crucial. What this seems to mean, Chris, is that the job with Hopkins and Jewell was a turning point in Natalie's life. She had no qualms about sending them a resumé and references, but once she was on their payroll, she wanted that information to go no further."

"And she moved in the middle of the month, as though she couldn't wait to get out of the Gramercy Park apartment," I added. "Maybe he came back. Maybe she married—or knew—this man in her early to mid twenties, got away from him, moved to New York, thought she was free of him. Then one day she sees him, or he finds her and she becomes terrified. She changes jobs, moves, leaves no forwarding address, hoping to escape from him."

"It would seem she did for five years."

"And then he saw her at the parade," I said, feeling a shiver.

"What do you know about this man Martin Jewell?"

"Only that he seems very successful at his job, that he and his partner started with very little and have built up a lucrative business. Do you think he could be involved in this?"

"He sounds like a man who piles his plate a little too high. I'm sure there are men who manage to maintain several relationships at one time, but from where I sit, it sounds as though it can't be easy." She pulled a sheet of paper closer to her. "Let's see who we have. The husband, of course, although both you and Jack don't think he's a serious candidate for murder. The nameless abusive husband or lover who's been after her for years. Or, as you suggested, perhaps a fitting but unexciting husband that she simply wanted to get away from."

"In which case she's still alive somewhere."

"Certainly a happier ending," Joseph said. "Then there's the elusive brother or lover who may be named Terry. It would certainly be nice to find him, wouldn't it?"

"He might know a great deal about her, and if he cared, he would help. But I have no idea where to look or even if his last name is Miller."

Joseph picked up the ring of keys. "I'm still bothered, Chris. I'm not sure I can put into words what it is, but this house key is a problem for me."

"I'll call the super when I get home."

* * *

It wasn't as easy as picking up the phone. I hadn't gotten the super's name and it hadn't occurred to me to ask for her phone number. But a call to Dickie Foster gave me both and a call to Mrs. Franco gave me the additional information that Joseph wanted.

"Sure she gave us the key. I can't remember now whether she handed it to me or left it in the apartment, but I got it back."

"Was it an original or a copy?" I asked.

"I don't know. It looked like the real thing to me."

I thanked her and was hanging up when she said, "You still there?"

"Yes. Is there something else?"

"I was talking to my husband about Natalie after you were here. He said some guy came around a couple of years ago asking about her."

"Really? Asking what?"

"Where she moved to. Rich didn't tell him because he didn't know and the guy left."

"Did he leave a name or address?"

"I don't think so, but he said he was Natalie's brother."

Interesting. "Thanks for telling me, Mrs. Franco." The news gave me a chill. Maybe someone had been looking for her for a long time, someone up to no good.

I didn't bother telling her I still had a key that opened that door. When this was all over I would see to it that the key was returned.

The next day I taught my class, came home, and prepared my lesson for the following Tuesday, just in case something happened and I didn't have much time. It turned out to be lucky that I did.

Late in the afternoon Sandy called. "I just got a response," he said, but he didn't sound happy. "It was a man's voice. He said, 'You'll never find her.' "

19

"So it wasn't much of a conversation," Jack said.

"It was very short." He had just come home and we were at the kitchen table, as usual. "He picked up the phone—he's been answering it since yesterday morning without letting calls go through his secretary—and a man said, 'You looking for Natalie Miller?' and he said he was and asked if the man had any information. And the man said, 'She's been missing since Thanksgiving Day two years ago and you'll never find her.' "

"That sounds like our man. You didn't mention Thanksgiving Day in the ad, did you?"

"No, but the people I've talked to know that's when she disappeared."

"But they don't know you put an ad in an Indiana newspaper."

"Only you and Sandy know."

"And there's no way of knowing if the call came from Indiana or next door."

"No way that I can think of."

"I suppose it's too much to ask if he recognized an accent or an age in the voice."

"He said the only thing he was sure of was that it was male and he spoke English."

"Look, Chris, it means you're in the right area. Either this guy read your ad or someone out there read it and told him about it. Either way, there's a connection between Natalie Miller and that part of Indiana."

"But thousands of people must have read those newspapers. Why should the only person to call be someone who wishes Natalie ill?"

"I can't answer that. Let me make a suggestion. I've been thinking about the fact that she changed her looks. There was a forensic sculptor that used to work at the Police Academy years ago. He was actually a sergeant for a long time and there was some trouble, I don't know the details, and he retired kind of suddenly and left New York. He lives somewhere over in Broome County on the southern tier—I can get his address from the Pension Section—and maybe you can use your charm on him."

"I don't understand. Don't these people take a picture of someone a long time ago and project what they'd look like today?"

"Sure, but they can do the reverse, too. They can take what you look like today and go back in time to when you were younger."

"So someone in Indiana who doesn't recognize today's Natalie might recognize her as a high school graduate."

"Right."

"You seem to think it'll be tough getting him to talk to me."

"From what I've heard, he lives alone in a shack that isn't much better than a chicken coop. A guy I know once made a trip out there to see him and he was turned away pretty nastily."

I looked across the table at him. "Where did we leave the book on charm? I think I have some serious reading to do."

"Honey, you've got charm written all over you. You think I married you for your short hair and master's degree in English?"

My hair had been little more than a bristle when I'd left

St. Stephen's and only half an inch longer than that when I met Jack at the Sixty-fifth Precinct. "I never thought of myself as charming," I said.

"Hey, that's why you've got me. To let you know how terrific you are."

Marriage is a never-ending wonder.

Jack called his friend in the morning and got both meticulous directions to Sergeant Albert DiMartino's little house and a strong caution on DiMartino's personality. "I'll translate it into polite language because you don't want to hear the original," Jack said when he got off the phone. "He says the guy acts like a rotten bastard."

"And that's the clean version."

"Very clean. My friend was really ticked. He made the trip with Al's best interests at heart—he thought Al got a raw deal on the job—and Al wouldn't open his door. I'm having second thoughts about you going there, but my recollection is, he was always very nice to women, probably too nice."

"If he doesn't open his door, there isn't much chance of trouble."

"I guess that means you're going."

"I'm also packing a bag. There must be a motel around the area. I'll check with Sandy before I go. But I may not get home tonight."

"Here we go again, huh?"

"You know I'll miss you."

"Just keep calling, OK?"

"You couldn't stop me."

Sandy was all for it. He asked if my expense fund needed an infusion and I said I'd let him know. I hadn't been billed for the newspaper ads yet, so I hadn't drawn all that much out of the bank. Before I left, I put the rest of the expense money in our checking account so I could pay a

motel bill if I had to. I called Mel and told her where I was
going.

"A forensic sculptor?" she said in surprise. "Where is all
this leading?"

"I hope to someone who knows or knew Natalie. Our ad
in an Indiana paper got a response." I described it and she
gasped. "So I'll be going to Broome County in a little
while."

"Poor Jack."

"I know. But he put me up to this. I think he gets as
much of a kick as I do when I turn up something."

"Happy landings."

Route 17 took me right into Broome County, and then
the directions Jack had written down took over. On a road
that was generously considered secondary, I finally spotted
Cowles's Fruit Orchard, alerting me that I had a turn coming up. It seemed impossible, but the next road was in
worse shape than the last one, pitted and rutted, so narrow
I would have to move off it onto a nonexistent shoulder if
anyone approached, which was not very likely. The next
landmark was a sign that said PROCEED AT OWN RISK, but
that sign had not survived. It lay defeated in the scrub at
the side of the road, a victim, perhaps, of Al DiMartino
himself in a fit of anger, or of a windstorm or a large an-
imal on a dark night. I slowed to a crawl, searching the left
side of the road for Mr. DiMartino's "driveway." Even so,
I missed it, realizing only after my front wheels had over-
shot it that the track into the woods and brush was the
"drive."

I backed up and turned sharply, my first real fears mate-
rializing as I pulled into the narrow opening. I would have
missed it completely if not for the tire treads imprinted in
the snow. I drove slowly, encountering no obstructions, and
suddenly, ahead of me, there was a clearing with a small

wooden structure on the right and a car parked in a kind of lean-to tacked onto the right-hand side.

I left my car in the clearing and got out. The front door must have been the only entrance, because there were footprints and trampled snow between it and the carport. It was so quiet that I was sure he must have heard my car pull up, but there was no sound from inside either. I walked up to the door, looked for a bell, and then, laughing at my naïveté, knocked loudly. There was no answer.

I knocked again and called, "Mr. DiMartino?"

"Go away," an angry man's voice came back at me. "I don't give directions."

"I want to talk to you."

"I don't speak the language."

I smiled. "Well, I'll speak yours."

Suddenly the curtain in the window of the door was pulled aside. "What the hell do you want?"

"I want to talk to you. I'm told you're a forensic sculptor."

"Get outa here." The curtain closed and I heard him walk away.

"I need your services, Sergeant," I said.

"Leave me alone. You're bothering me."

"It's cold out here. Could I just come in and warm up?"

"No!"

I hadn't been exaggerating. I was freezing. If he didn't let me inside pretty soon, I was going to have to get in the car and warm myself up or drive somewhere warm. "I have something very interesting for you, Sergeant DiMartino. Would you just give me ten minutes to tell you about it?"

In answer I saw the twin barrels of a shotgun on the other side of the window.

I backed away off to the side. Maybe he really was crazy and I had made a terrible mistake coming here. I thought he was an embittered man living alone; I hadn't imagined he

was crazy enough to shoot an unarmed stranger. It occurred
to me that my car might well be within range of his gun,
and if he shot out a couple of my tires, I would have one
terrible hike in the cold back to the orchard.

I leaned against the front of the house so he could not
see me without opening the door. Somehow I thought he
just wanted to scare me away, not come out in the cold and
do me harm. I also didn't think he really wanted to shoot
through his window on a day as cold as this. Since I had
come in a car, he would know I was still here as long as
the car was parked in front of his windows. I thought about
my next move and came up with nothing. If I drove to the
road and walked back to the house, I would surprise him,
but what good would that do? It was unlikely he had a
phone, so going somewhere and calling was out of the
question. He could wear me down much easier than the reverse. I knew he had heat inside because I had seen smoke
from somewhere as I approached, and as I stood there I
smelled some woodsmoke as the wind shifted. Ergo he
could hold out forever while I froze to death.

I was really cold now and I was torn between waiting for
him to change his mind because of my persistence and at-
tending to my needs. Frostbite wasn't going to improve my
life, and my fingers and toes were already complaining. I
inched back to the door. The curtain was in place and there
was no sign of the shotgun. He had put it aside and was ig-
noring me.

"Sergeant DiMartino," I called.

"Get offa my property."

"I'm looking for a woman who's disappeared. I need
someone to make a sculpture for me and I've been told
you're the best."

"I'm retired. Leave me alone."

"I'm prepared to pay you well for your services."

There was silence. I had been prepared all along to pay
him, but I had hoped he would agree to talk to me before

the question of money came up. Having worked so many years for a stipend that never exceeded a hundred dollars a month, I sometimes have difficulty judging value. But this man might genuinely need money. I didn't know the particulars of his problems with the police department, and I had no idea whether he was living on an adequate pension. Judging from his digs, he might not be.

I waited in the silent cold, hoping he would change his mind. I gave him ten frigid minutes, but nothing happened. "Sergeant?" I called. "Can we talk about it?"

"Come back tomorrow. I'm busy today."

"Will you do it then? Will you talk to me?"

"I don't know."

Was it the money or was it the challenge? It was already too late for me to drive back to Oakwood. I hadn't seen the sun for hours because of the overcast sky, but now it was getting darker and I didn't want to drive unfamiliar snowy roads at night. It looked as though I was going to have to find a motel and make a decision tomorrow about what else to do.

Suddenly he called something, but I missed it. "What did you say?" I called back. I really hated this shouting match.

"How much you paying?"

"We have to talk about it."

"I'm not letting you in till I'm sure I want to."

"Tell me what you charge."

"Tell me what you're paying."

A standoff where I'm out in the cold and he's inside where it's warm is not my idea of equal opportunity. I thought quickly about how much of Sandy's money I had left. "Two hundred," I called.

"Forget it."

So we were going to have to bargain. I am not good at this, I thought miserably. What if he wanted thousands? I couldn't commit Sandy to a fortune. "Two fifty," I responded.

There was silence. I waited, wondering if I would ever feel my toes again. "Three hundred," I said, "and that's my last offer. I'm freezing out here and I have to get somewhere warm."

Silence again. What am I doing here? I asked myself. This is a man who wouldn't even let an old friend in, someone who cared enough about him to make the trip from New York. I walked over to the car and got in. From there I could see the whole front of the house, but all the windows were curtained and I couldn't see inside. If he had some special viewing place, I couldn't detect it. I put the key in the ignition and started the motor. The car was facing the wrong way and I would have to swing around in a U to get back on the narrow path to the road. DiMartino didn't have that problem. I could see where his tire tracks were; he backed up and turned toward the road easily.

I started forward, making a wide swing to my left, away from the house, pushing through snow that was fairly high. But it was too much for the car, which ground to a stop as I felt the beginnings of panic. I didn't want to have to leave my car here as I begged for help from the orchard a mile down the road, where the farmer, if he had any sense at all, would have left for a warmer climate weeks ago.

I backed up and tried again with no luck. I turned the motor off and got out. Thanks to Jack, I kept a small snow shovel in the trunk and a container of sand. The sand wasn't necessary at this point, but the shovel might do the trick. I started working at it, but it was tough going and I stood back to survey the terrain and catch my breath. That's when it occurred to me I was doing everything backward. I got in the car and backed up as nearly as I could in my own tracks till I reached the ruts DiMartino had made as he backed out of the carport. Slowly I moved the car till it nearly touched the back of his. Then I went forward in his path into the carport.

I paused to let the system rest. It had been both physically and spiritually taxing. As I recovered, I heard something and I turned around. DiMartino was standing outside his door, waving to me. I inched the car forward to make sure I could continue and got out.

"Come here," he called. "What you doin' that for?"

"You told me to get off your property. I was getting off."

"Come inside before you freeze to death."

Thanks, I thought. I'm already three-quarters there.

The house was one large room, more like a studio apartment in New York than a place to live in the country. And it was clearly an artist's studio. Although there was a bed off to one side and what looked like a kitchen against the back wall, the rest of the space was covered with sculpture. I didn't know how the man got from one piece to another, so close were they to each other. And centered in the large room was a stove with a chimney rising through the roof.

It was actually hot inside. I waited a minute, then unbuttoned my coat with stiff fingers, pulled off my gloves, and finally took the coat off. He didn't offer to take it, so I made my way to the bed and left it there.

"Who are you?" DiMartino said.

"Chris Bennett. My husband is a detective sergeant at the Sixty-fifth."

"The Six-five. I know the Six-five. What's his name?"

"Jack Brooks."

"Brooks. I remember him. He's OK."

I thought he was a little better than that, but this wasn't the time to promote the man I loved. "He said you were the best."

"A lot of good it did me."

"I need your help."

"Yeah."

That seemed the end of the conversation. DiMartino reached for an open bottle of liquor and poured some into a water glass, looking questioningly at me as he did so. When I shook my head, he drank some.

"I drink a little," he said.

It didn't come as a surprise. He settled back in his chair. I found another one next to his bed and dragged it to the center of the room. DiMartino looked like a man who had given up all those little things we take pains to do to show ourselves we are civilized human beings. His clothes were less than clean and he wore them sloppily. His hair, which was receding, was too long and choppily cut, as though he took a chunk from here and a chunk from there when it suited him or when he got tired of looking at it in the mirror. He had a gut, which must have made it hard to chop wood, and that seemed to be the fuel of choice in his stove.

"You know what they did to me?"

"Jack said you got a raw deal."

"I was always a little outspoken, said what I thought when I thought it. I had a little disagreement with my lieutenant about some evidence, and later on I got cornered by a reporter. So I told him what I thought, which wasn't what everybody else thought, and the dummy quoted me and printed my name and it got back to the guy who runs the lab."

"You mean they fired you for expressing an opinion?" I could feel my ire rise.

"Nobody fired me. They just piled up a lot of junk against me." He had started to speak more carefully, his diction more correct, as though he might be a man not afraid to show the effects of education. It was hard for me to believe it was this same man who had shouted "Get outa here" only an hour ago. "Then one day I took a piece of evidence from the property room, checked it out with the clerk, and forgot to get it back in time. I put it in my locker overnight and the next morning they said I'd stolen it."

"How terrible."

"Right. How terrible. Something people do all the time, only that time they wanted me, so it became a violation of department rules and procedures. I had a great choice, sit in a radio car in Brooklyn for two years or retire."

"It really was a raw deal."

"So here I am. My wife left me and I'm living the life of Riley in Broome County. Sure you don't want a drink?"

"I'm positive."

"So you want me to help you find someone."

"She disappeared at the Thanksgiving Day parade the year before last. The police haven't found her and a private detective hasn't found her. I'm looking as a favor to her family."

"You have pictures?"

"Out in the car."

"Let's take a look."

20

It was dark when I left. The transformation that had taken over DiMartino had been wonderful to watch. As his speech had changed, so did his demeanor. Before my eyes he went from the sloppy, angry hermit to the consummate professional. He looked at the pictures with a magnifying glass he found in a desk almost hidden behind sculptures. He looked at the dentist's report and the hair swatches I had gotten from the hairdresser. He listened to everything I had to say and took notes.

"Probably made herself over," he grumbled at one point. Then he went back to the pictures.

Finally he asked if I would leave everything with him overnight and we would talk in the morning.

"I'll bring breakfast," I said. "What time do you open for business?"

He gave me the first hesitant smile of my visit. "Eight o'clock for breakfast. Work as soon as we're finished eating. Bring an extra coffee."

I said I would and I drove into town and got myself a room for the night.

I was back at the stroke of eight. He had shoveled in front of the carport so there was room for me to park. As I reached the door, he opened it.

"Come on in. I've cleared a place where we can sit."

The place was a table in the kitchen area. Yesterday it

164

had been buried under what looked to me like debris, but one man's art is another's debris, as most of us have learned. We sat and ate a hearty breakfast with eggs and sausage and muffins, juice and coffee.

"Better when someone else cooks it," he said.

"Jack sends his regards. He told me you were always nice to women."

"Most cops are."

I thought that was rather gallant, considering. "I think we have some business to conduct before we go on." I had talked to Sandy last night, and he was willing to spend more than I had imagined on this project.

"We'll talk business later. I was up most of the night working. Come over here."

I had wanted to clean up the table first, but he had no time for that. He led me to a cloth-covered object set about shoulder height and pulled the sheet off. A white, bald-headed Natalie looked at me.

"I can't believe it," I said.

"It needs the right wig and I don't have one. Do you have a scarf?"

I got the long wool scarf that I wrapped around my neck in cold weather. He put it over Natalie's head and crossed it along the front of her neck.

"It's fantastic," I said.

"It needs some color, but I'll take care of that later. I use white clay and I don't fire it. If you're going to fire it, you have to cut it open around here—" he pointed to the place where the eyebrows would be "—and scoop out the inside so it'll dry, which takes a few weeks, and I figure you want this yesterday. You're using this for photos, right?"

"Right," I said. "And I have her cosmetics. Her husband gave them to me." I took a small plastic bag out of my shoulder bag and gave it to him. Her lipsticks were in there, her foundation, her powder.

"This is good, gives me an idea of her color preferences." He took the foundation and smeared it on the white clay face and it sprang to life. I half expected to see the lips move, to hear Natalie's voice.

"It must be the Pinocchio syndrome," I said. "I thought I saw her move."

This time I got a real smile. "I live with these guys. They're pretty quiet."

"Where do we go from here?"

"From here I take her back. You said you couldn't find anything about her before five years ago. I think she made herself over, straightened her teeth, capped the bad ones, changed her hairstyle and color. I've been looking at that nose and I can almost give you the name of the plastic surgeon."

"You think she had her nose fixed?"

"I'm almost sure of it. I think she made herself from a plain little girl, maybe even a homely little girl, into a good-looking woman."

"How old do you think she is?"

"I could be off, but I'd say thirty-eight, forty."

That was Susan Hartswell's guess, more or less. "What will you take her back to?"

"Say, twenty years. The people who went to high school with her will remember her. That's what you want, isn't it?"

"I want the person who may have kidnapped her. Maybe her old high school friends can put me onto him."

"Can I make a suggestion you won't like?"

"Go on. I'll take all the professional help I can get."

"Have you checked out the husband?"

"The detective who inherited the case checked him out and seemed convinced it was a happy marriage, and there were no rumors about him. He really acts as though he wants to find her."

"Because he's the guy to check out first. It could be he never took her to the parade."

"There's a picture of her in the crowd."

"It's easy to take a picture in a crowd. You see the strip of negatives with the balloons in the one before her and the one after her?"

I hadn't. I shook my head.

"Could have been taken at a baseball game. You have to see if the people in the crowd fit, if the clothes are right for the time of year. Little things like that can tell you a lot."

"I don't think he did it," I said. "He got a phone call the other day from someone who read the ad I put in the paper."

"How do you know he got a phone call? Because he told you? If I'd killed my wife, I'd tell you the same thing. But I'd come up with a better story."

"I see what you mean," I said, feeling uncomfortable.

"You're a nice girl. Jack Brooks did himself a favor when he married you. You've got a good face, too, nice bone structure."

"Me?"

"You. OK. The question was, where do we go from here? From here on, I work alone. You give me your phone number, and when I have something to show you, I call you. There's nothing you can do here except look over my shoulder, and I don't work that way."

"So I go home."

"And wait for my call."

"You want me to leave the pictures?"

"I tell you what. Take the wedding album. Leave the rest. They're safe here."

"Then I'll be going." I got my coat and put it on. Then I turned and looked at the sculpted face with the lipstick. It was about to undergo what a lot of people would sell a soul for, taking off twenty years. "You seem in a much better mood today, Sergeant," I said.

"It's like Jack told you. I'm nice to women."

* * *

I called Sandy in midafternoon when I reached home. He sounded ecstatic, almost as though his missing wife were on the verge of being delivered to his doorstep. I had very little hope that that would ever happen.

Jack listened to my story when he came home from law school. "So it's really remote," he said after my description of DiMartino's house.

"I doubt whether he sees anyone besides the people in the supermarket and the bank."

"And he probably picks up his mail at the post office. Does he have a phone?"

"I didn't see one, but he said he'd call me when I should come back for the sculptures. Was he a drinker when you knew him?"

"It's not unheard-of for a guy on the job to take a sip now and then."

"This was more than that. He kept an open bottle where he could reach it. Though this morning I noticed it wasn't there. I think he was energized by having an assignment, especially one he'd be paid for."

"Work does magic. So what's the game plan?"

"I guess I just sit and wait for DiMartino's call. I've followed up on just about everything I can. The next move has to be another ad in the Indiana paper with the picture of Natalie as a nineteen- or twenty-year-old. If she grew up there, there have to be people who remember her. There has to be a high school yearbook with a picture that'll be close to what DiMartino's going to give me."

"So we wait for the phone to ring."

"It won't be the first time."

On Friday morning I decided to talk to Sandy for the first time about Natalie's mysterious "brother."

"Of course you're not bothering me," he said over the phone. "I always have time for this. Is something up?"

I told him about my conversations with Dickie Foster

and the super at Natalie's former apartment near Gramercy Park.

"She had no brothers," he said. "No brothers and no sisters. The feeling I got, although she never came out and said it, was that she was illegitimate, given up by her mother, and raised by a foster family. Whether they were related by blood or not, I wasn't sure from the way she told it."

"But you know, if her natural mother married later, she might have had more children that would be related to Natalie."

"She was pretty emphatic about being an only child."

"The question is who this man is. Maybe he's the abusive husband we've talked about."

"Whoever he is, this is confirmation that you're on the right track, Chris. I think when that sculpture is done, we're going to get some answers."

It turned out, eventually, that he was right. But the answers we got were to questions we had never asked.

Just as I was about to go out to do some necessary shopping, the phone rang. An operator was at the other end.

"I have a call from Mabel Bernstein in Antigua," she said. "Will you pay for the call?"

"Yes, I will." There was a little static and then I said, "Mrs. Bernstein?"

"Christine?"

"Yes, it's me. How's your vacation?"

"Warm and wonderful. I remembered something that may help you."

"I'm all ears."

"Natalie went away one weekend—can you hear me all right?"

"I hear you fine."

"She went away with a friend," she continued, straining her voice. "A man friend. And she wrote me a postcard.

She said she was having a great time and he was a real jewel."

"A jewel?" I repeated. "Like a diamond?"

"Yes. That kind of jewel."

"Do you remember when she wrote it to you?"

"Early on. Probably the first year she lived on Greenwich Avenue."

"Mrs. Bernstein, do you remember where it was mailed from?"

"Yes. It came from one of those lakes or something upstate."

"Upstate in what state?" I asked.

"New York. I bet it was Saratoga Springs or one of those places."

"You're sure it didn't come from New Jersey?"

"I haven't lost all my marbles yet. It came from New York. I may even have the card somewhere at home, but I'm not going to be home for another month."

"Thank you for keeping this in mind. This has really been very helpful."

"Did you expect New Jersey?"

"I did."

"Does this put a monkey wrench in your investigation?"

"No. It just means someone's memory wasn't as good as yours."

"You mean he lied, don't you?"

"It's possible. Enjoy the tropics, Mrs. Bernstein. And keep in touch if you remember anything else."

I took myself off to the supermarket to think about what I had learned. Martin Jewell had been absolutely certain he and Natalie had gone to Cape May and that he had chosen the spot. When someone lies to me with such conviction, I am naturally alert. As I pushed my cart through the aisles, loading it in preparation for our weekend, I asked myself whether I wanted to challenge Jewell's statement, whether it was important, whether he had just become a suspect in Natalie's disappearance because they had spent a weekend in one place instead of another.

By the time I got home, I knew I had to call him. The person who answered the phone gave me a little trouble but relented and put me through.

"Yes, how are you?" Martin Jewell's voice said. "Any news on Natalie?"

"Something has come up," I answered, avoiding the question. "It seems Natalie sent a friend a postcard the weekend you and she went away."

"Uh-huh."

"And it looks like you didn't go to Cape May."

"Sure we did. I always—" He stopped. Then he mumbled something under his breath that might have been an obscenity. "You're right, we didn't. We went to New York State. North, not south."

"Do you remember the place?"

"It was a hotel. I don't remember the name of it. It was five years ago."

"Was it her idea to go there?"

"It must have been. I always pick Cape May. I mean when I go away for the weekend."

"Do you remember the town?"

"It was north of Albany, around Saratoga Springs, I think. It was a hell of a drive."

"Do you know why she picked that place?"

"If she told me, I don't remember. It was a nice place, though, now that I think about it, a country inn or something, fireplace in every room kind of thing."

"Anything else you remember? Did you visit anyone she knew?"

"We didn't spend much time sightseeing," he said, as though instructing me on the purpose of the trip. "Wait a minute. I do remember something." He sounded eager.

"She got up in the middle of the night and went somewhere."

"Alone?"

"Without me anyway. I woke up and she wasn't there. She walked in, fully dressed, a little while later, said she couldn't sleep and had gone out for a walk. But I think she took my car."

"She drove somewhere?"

"There was more mileage on it than I remembered. My keys were on the dresser. She could have taken them with no trouble."

"Thank you very much, Mr. Jewell."

"No problem."

"Let me know if anything else occurs to you."

He was awfully smooth. He was so believable, I found myself believing him, as I had before. Maybe he had made an honest mistake. Maybe he usually weekended at Cape May and it had slipped his mind where he and Natalie had gone together. It was, as he had said, five years ago.

I decided to set Natalie Miller Gordon aside for the weekend.

21

Elsie Rivers called over the weekend, a nice, homey kind of call, how good it was to see me again, to meet my husband, how memories of my mother had come back to her after we left, bringing her joy. We chatted for some time, discussing when we might get together again, although we never picked a date, and when I got off the phone I had that feeling again, that there was something she knew, something she was thinking about telling me but couldn't quite bring herself to do it.

"Sounded like your mom's old friend," Jack said when I had hung up. "She say anything?"

"She came close, Jack. She wants to and she doesn't want to. I wish I'd never remembered this."

"Whatever it is, it's long past."

"That's not a reason to forget it."

"But it's a reason to forgive."

"I have to know what I'm forgiving."

"Give her time. You've stirred up a lot of her past. She has to decide where her loyalties lie, or where they should lie."

"Do you think he met her at work? At one of the businesses he visited?"

"Chris, you don't know who she is. Don't jump to conclusions."

But I had made the leap and I didn't like where I found myself.

* * *

The quiet of the weekend came to an end on Monday.
Dickie Foster called in the morning.

"Remember that postcard I told you about? I found it."

"You must have worked all weekend," I said.

"Turned the whole place upside down. Now we'll have
to move because I've started throwing things out. Any nice
little houses out your way?"

"Plenty. Come up and take a look some weekend. Tell
me about the postcard."

"It says, 'Dear Dickie, It's gorgeous up here. Can't wait
for the job interview. I'm taking some time to rest up so
I'm in good form. Yours, Natalie.' "

"Where's it from?"

"The picture says Lake George, but the postmark—it's a
little hard to read, but I think it's Saratoga."

"Upstate New York."

"That's what it looks like."

"Dickie, I can't thank you enough. Will you hang on to
the card? I may want to look at it later."

"I'll put it away so it doesn't get mixed up with the
trash. I'm really glad I found it. Brings back those good old
days when I was single."

Something had drawn Natalie to upstate New York twice
in about a year, once before she moved out of Gramercy
Park and once when she and Jewell went off for a weekend
together. Was there an old lover up there, a husband and
children, or the mysterious abuser whom I had come to believe in? Maybe she had been drawn to him as I had read
many women are even when their intellects tell them they
should stay away. But I was certain now that there was a
connection between her and some place in Saratoga or Warren County.

I had lunch and took a walk, having missed my early
walk this morning. In the winter, later walks were easier

because the temperature was higher and there was a chance of sun. Today the sun was shining and I was glad I had postponed, not eliminated, my gentle exercise.

Back home, I put my house in order. I find that when I'm consumed with my work, whether it's an investigation or something I'm doing for Arnold or the college, things get a little disorganized and I appreciate some downtime to reestablish order. I gathered up newspapers and put them in bags for the recycling program, then hauled out the vacuum cleaner, going from room to room without stopping, the momentum carrying me through. When I finished and went downstairs, I found the answering machine was flashing, the ring of the phone having been obscured by the noise I was generating. I pushed the PLAY button and heard a startling message.

"Miss Bennett, this is Arlene Hopkins. I think we got off on the wrong foot when we spoke a couple of weeks ago. Would you call me on my private line as soon as possible?" She dictated a number that I had to listen to a second time with a paper and pencil in my hand. Then I called it.

"This is Arlene," the voice answered.

"This is Chris Bennett."

"Yes, I'm so glad you called. Are you free for dinner tonight?"

Jack was at law school and I had already done all my work for my poetry class last week. "Yes, I am."

"Come to my apartment, OK?"

"That's fine."

"You can park right in the building. I'll tell them to save a space for you." She gave me an address on East Sixty-third Street and I promised to be there at seven.

Then I called Jack and let him know.

New York is many worlds. It's a cliché to say that the richest and poorest people in the country live there, but it's a dramatic truth when you see it for yourself. Arlene

Hopkins was neither, but she certainly tended more to the brighter end of the spectrum. My car was accepted courteously and I went up to the lobby level and found the elevator that would take me to her apartment, passing through security first. I half expected to be asked to turn out my pockets and submit to a metal detector, but the uniformed man let me through with a tight smile after comparing my name with one on a list. I rode up a swift elevator to the eleventh floor and found Arlene Hopkins out in the corridor, awaiting me.

"Come on in," she said cordially, her voice and dress so different from what I had encountered in her office that I wondered whether she might be the good twin. "I'll take your coat. We can have a drink in the living room before we sit down."

The apartment was spectacular. One wall of the huge living room was mostly glass, and the view, unobscured, was south with glimpses of Central Park to the west and to the east of the East River.

"It's very beautiful," I said. I was wearing a brown pants outfit that I considered more than casual, but my hostess was in tight black pants and a white silk blouse with ruffles and frills that seemed out of character for the woman in the pin-striped suit at the office.

"I enjoy living here. What will you drink?" Canapés were already out on a table with white cocktail napkins imprinted with ARH in a small pile near them.

"White wine would be fine." I had noticed a bottle on her bar and decided I could tolerate a glass or two before driving home.

She took care of it all quickly and sat down in a chair and crossed her legs as though she was used to being comfortable there. "We got off to a bad start," she said, repeating what she had said on the answering machine. "I had a lot of reasons not to want to answer your questions. Those reasons are moot now, and I want to be open and forthright.

I know you suspect me of having done something duplicitous."

"I don't suspect you at all. I've had time to think over what I've learned, and I've learned a great deal since I spoke to you."

"Let me explain anyway. You've heard we're breaking up, haven't you?"

"Yes. I'm sorry and surprised."

"It's probably been incubating for a long time. If you think divorce is tough, you should try splitting a company in two. But he has his lawyer and I have mine, and things will work out somehow. The reason I was less than forthcoming is that I was afraid of losing Martin and the company."

"Ms. Hopkins—"

"Arlene, please. May I call you Chris?"

"Of course."

"Let's be as informal as we can. We'll never see each other again after tonight, but I have the feeling neither you nor I will ever forget this meeting."

The way she said it gave me a chill. "I don't need or want to hear about your personal life. What I'm interested in is finding Natalie Gordon, dead or alive. If you know anything, please tell me."

"I had a feeling about her," she said, leaning back comfortably, "a feeling that she was trying to upgrade herself, that she was a hick intent on learning to be a big-city woman, and the person she picked to imitate was me."

"How do you mean?"

"She would ask me about my cosmetics, my perfume, the name of the company that made my bags and shoes, and then she would turn up with not exactly the same things but similar ones. She left her lipstick in the ladies' room once and I picked it up, thinking it was mine. She wore a pair of shoes once that I recognized as this winter's update of the pair I had bought last winter."

"She admired you," I said. "You're a gorgeous woman and you dress magnificently." I had no intention of complimenting her; I was merely stating what was clearly true, but she nearly blushed as I said it. "She was a small-town girl from nowhere and you were the big-city success."

"I hope you don't flatter everyone this way."

"I don't and it isn't flattery."

"Maybe I saw myself in her then," Arlene said thoughtfully. "I have a reputation for being driven and I worked hard to earn it. I have to succeed; there are things I need that other people merely want. I can't relinquish control unless I have absolute confidence in the person I hand over the control to. Marty is one of the few." She took a sip of her drink. "Was."

I really didn't want to hear a recap of her love affair. "Tell me about Natalie."

"I hated her from the moment I saw her."

I took another canapé and a sip of wine. A woman men loved and women hated. "But you agreed to hire her."

"Marty wanted her and she would work for him more than for me. Wormy thought she was hot stuff. Her resumé was great, her references golden. I didn't steal them, Chris. I had no reason to. Nor did I 'borrow' them. And Wormy's clean. She leaves that office at night and becomes a mother. She doesn't think till the next morning."

A bell rang and I looked toward the sound.

"That's dinner. Grab a couple more and bring your glass along."

I followed her over the thick carpet into a kitchen that rivaled the Gordons', except that it was smaller. She put down her glass and opened a microwave oven. Out came two marvelous-looking Cornish hens, stuffed, with vegetables on the side.

"Want to take my glass in?"

"Sure." I picked up her drink and followed her into the

dining room. The table was glass and steel and set with place mats, fine china, sterling silver, and crystal.

"It's beautiful," I said.

"I like nice things."

Nice things was an understatement. We sat opposite each other and she went back for a bottle of bubbly water and the bottle of wine.

"Marty and I met seven years ago," she said when we were eating. "It happened. He's married and I didn't care. Having children isn't at the top of my list of priorities. Also I like living alone. At some point, we realized we were potentially a team in more ways than one. That's when Hopkins and Jewell was born. We had a good run and it's over. Someday someone'll write a book about it, but it won't be me.

"But it's Natalie you're interested in," she said, getting back on track with, I thought, some reluctance. She wanted to talk about the relationship; she would continue to make lots of money doing what she enjoyed doing, but she would miss the man. I could sympathize with her.

"Right," I said.

"She walked in dripping this sleazy sexuality and I knew Marty would fall for it. I suffered in advance, if you want to know the truth."

"But you didn't voice an objection."

"I knew what Marty would say if I did. And Wormy thought she was just what we needed. She was, in fact. She was terrific. There wasn't anything she wouldn't do. If I'd asked her to scrub a floor, she probably would've gotten down on her hands and knees. But Marty wanted to bed her, and she had no objections. I honestly think he thought I didn't know."

"But you knew before it happened."

"And I kept my mouth shut through the whole affair. We had a business relationship that had to be preserved at all costs. And we preserved it until a couple of weeks ago."

"Tell me about Natalie."

"She was a girl who came to town to make it. I don't think she gave much of a damn whether she did it on her own or married it. She thought Marty was her ticket to happiness. I knew he wasn't. If he hadn't left his wife for me, he wouldn't do it for Natalie. There was much less to Natalie than there was to me, and much less than met the eye. I had a feeling she was older than she said and anxious to land a man ASAP."

"Why didn't she leave H and J when the relationship ended?"

"She often got to meet clients. She may have thought that would lead somewhere. It might have. I think she dated a few men who came down to the office."

"Tell me about the missing papers."

"I never touched them. I probably never looked at them after the first interview. I didn't care. I more or less heard they were missing and I heard Natalie was upset. But since I didn't like her, and since she'd taken my man, at least part-time, I was perfectly willing to look on the dark side of her. I figured she'd faked her background to get the job with us."

"Wormy remembers calling a previous employer and getting a glowing recommendation."

Arlene smiled. "Just goes to show how little I know."

"I thought that she was trying to block out a former life, possibly a husband and children, possibly an abusive man who might come looking for her."

"I hadn't thought of that. Your analysis is certainly more charitable than mine. So you think she took the papers so there'd be no record if someone came calling."

"Pretty much. This chicken is great. Did you cook it earlier and freeze it?"

"Good God no. I'm not sure how to turn the stove on. In Manhattan you pick up the phone and order anything you want and they deliver it. All I'm making tonight is the coffee."

"You have good phone numbers," I said. "Go on about Natalie."

"About why she stayed. I thought about it myself when it happened. Frankly, there are office romances every day of the week, and when they end, the people involved think more about whether they can get a better job somewhere else or whether they're better off staying put. A lot of them stay put and watch their ex do the same thing with someone else in the office. In Natalie's case I thought she might not want to go elsewhere because she had faked her references. She would want to stay at H and J long enough that we'd be her best reference. But if you're right that Wormy checked her out, then maybe she stayed because she liked the job. I think she did like the job and she got raises, so she was doing a lot better at the end than at the beginning. We all were."

"Let me ask you something. I've been hearing that someone calling himself Natalie's brother may have been looking for her before she disappeared. Would you know if such a person called H and J?"

"There's no way of knowing. If someone called and asked for her, they'd put him through and no one would ever know who called. You think that's who's responsible for her disappearance?"

"I think he may not be a brother but he may be the responsible one. He inquired at the place she lived before she moved to Greenwich Avenue."

"So he may have found her."

"I'm just not sure how, unless the Thanksgiving Day parade was an accidental meeting. The super in her old building didn't know where she'd moved."

"How did you find the old building if we didn't have the address?"

"I worked backwards. An old woman in the Greenwich

Avenue building remembered the name of the moving company."

"You're pretty resourceful. You looking for a job at an advertising agency run by a driven woman?"

I smiled, feeling flattered. "Probably not, but I'll let you know if I change my mind."

"Let's have dessert."

We talked about more general things for the rest of the evening. I hadn't learned much, but she had had the opportunity to clear herself of suspicion. And maybe she'd managed to get a few things off her chest. For my part, I saw her differently and I understood why she had been so difficult when I had first shown up at H and J.

We finished our coffee in the living room, sitting as we had when I had arrived. I walked over to the windows and looked at New York in the dark.

"You don't see the grubbiness from up here," Arlene said.

"It's really quite beautiful. Did you have any sense of where Natalie came from originally?"

"Probably not New York, but I couldn't tell you how long she'd lived here when she came to work for us."

"She'd lived in the old apartment at least two years and she'd had at least two jobs."

"I'm sorry about what happened to her. I didn't like the woman and she did things that hurt me, but I didn't wish her the kind of harm that's probably befallen her."

"I think we're going to find her," I said, looking her straight in the eye.

"Do you know where?"

"Not in the city. If you remember anything else about her, I'm still interested."

"I'll try."

"Thank you for a wonderful dinner and a wonderful evening."

She smiled. "The job offer was sincere."

I promised again I would consider it.

22

"So you think she cleared herself," Jack said as we talked about my evening later that night.

"She admitted she hated Natalie. If she'd had anything to do with Natalie's disappearance, I think she would never have said that to me."

"Maybe she just reads character pretty well and she figured how you'd react."

"Maybe. But she had no motive, Jack. When Martin Jewell was involved with Natalie, that's when Arlene had a motive. Three years later—that's hard to see."

"Let me ask you a potentially embarrassing question: If Natalie didn't make herself disappear, who've you got?"

It was embarrassing because I still didn't know whether Natalie had engineered her own disappearance, and if she hadn't, I had no real suspect and almost no one even marginally suspicious. "Sandy, of course, although I don't believe he did it, Martin Jewell because he had a close relationship with Natalie, and this mysterious 'brother' who has popped up a couple of times and, as far as Sandy is concerned, doesn't exist."

"And Arlene Hopkins."

"You see a smoldering resentment."

"No question about it. Four years ago she thought it was all over. Suddenly you appear on the scene, dragging up unpleasant and embarrassing facts. She has a knock-down-drag-out with Jewell that's so bad, they decide to go their separate ways. If she's still so touchy about Natalie, it's possible she just bided her time and got her at the parade. I'll bet your friend Arlene works out in a gym twice a week and is just as tough physically as she is in her office."

"I guess I just don't like to think of a woman as a killer."

"Your problem, my lovely wife, is that when someone invites you to her home and serves you up a good meal and good conversation, you give her the benefit of the doubt."

"So you've figured me out," I said with resignation.

"It's not bad. I like it. It's just you may be writing off a suspect."

I went off to teach my poetry class on Tuesday morning still thinking about Jack's comments on Arlene Hopkins. The class went well and when it was over I decided to stay and have lunch in the college cafeteria, which was much better than the usual institutional eatery, a direct result of a food service program at the college whose students prepared and served the food. On that Tuesday they offered a wonderful split pea soup, which I ate with saltine crackers and a glass of tomato juice, feeling warm and satisfied when I finished.

I got home to find our answering machine blinking and two messages recorded on the tape.

"This message is for Christine Bennett. This is Al DiMartino, Chris. Your busts are ready. I got them done and dried enough and I'm just working on the color now. Drive up any time. I'm always here."

The second message was from Jack. "Hiya, love of my life. Have I got news for you. Give me a call."

I dialed his number with a little nervousness. It was the kind of message that could mean information that might blow everything I had learned out of the water.

"Six-five Squad, Sergeant Brooks, can I help you?"

"I hope so," I said.

"Chris?"

"Is it good news or bad news?"

"Hell, I can never figure that out. But I love it. I did a little checking this morning after I got in. Your friend Arlene Hopkins? Guess what. She has a permit for a target gun."

"A license for a gun?" I was truly shocked.

"A target gun. They're different from regular handguns. They can be a single-shot precision tool, a .22-caliber or a regular .38 revolver, or a lot of other things."

"Do they hold killer bullets?"

"Sure do. But the law says she can't walk around with it in her handbag. She can keep it unloaded in a carry case in her car or in a case on her person between where she lives and the place she practices shooting, maybe a local range. Not that that would stop a determined killer."

"So she could have had it in her bag that Thanksgiving Day."

"You bet. She's been licensed for several years, three anyway. When was the disappearance? A year and a half ago?"

"Less."

"Well, there you have it, a suspect with the means and opportunity and a beauty of a motive."

"I can't believe it," I said.

"Believe it. She renewed the permit early, so she's a current license holder."

"And if she's as good at shooting as she seems to be at everything else, she's just become a suspect."

I told him about the call from DiMartino and we agreed that I would drive up early tomorrow and try to come home the same day. Then I called Sandy and told him I was picking up the busts and when I got them home, I'd need them photographed.

"I have a great camera," he said. "Call me when you get back and we'll set up a shooting session. It shouldn't take long. This model isn't going to complain about the pictures."

I said I'd call him and I went to the bank to take out cash for DiMartino. Besides his fee, he would probably have expenses for the materials he used.

I sat down at my desk with my classwork and started looking over the quizzes I'd popped at the end of the second hour. They were about what I usually got, a handful of good answers from a group of students who were prepared, a bunch of paragraphs that were written in English but bore no resemblance to answers to my questions from students who couldn't believe they could ever be asked a question without a week's warning, and three almost blank papers from students who probably shouldn't have registered for the course.

While I was working, the phone on the desk rang. When I picked it up, I got a big surprise.

"Is this Christine Bennett?" The voice was male, casual, upbeat, and one I had never heard before.

"Yes it is."

"Hi, how're ya doin'? This is Ted Miller, Natalie's brother."

"Who?" I asked, not believing my own ears.

"I'm Natalie Miller's brother. I heard you were looking for her."

"Where did you get my name and phone number?" No name had been listed in the ad, and only Sandy's phone number.

"Let's just say I have a friend on a paper in Indiana."

"I see." I was struggling to think of the right thing to say. If this was really her brother, I could confide in him—maybe. But if this was a husband, abusive or otherwise, I wanted to keep him as far from me as possible, and if he had my name and phone number from a "friend" on a newspaper, he might also have my address as well. "Do you know where she is?" I asked.

"Haven't got the faintest. Do you?"

"No I don't."

"Well, I've been looking for her for a long time and I haven't come up with anything. You get any responses to your ad?"

"Nothing useful. Are you the person who made inquiries at Natalie's old apartment?"

"What place was that?"

"I don't have the address handy." And it didn't sound like he was the one. "How do I know you're her brother?"

"I'll send you my birth certificate if you want."

"Where were you born?"

"Just outside of Indianapolis. Same place Natalie was born. She's my big sister."

"Did she live in Connersville?"

"Sure did. We grew up there."

"Then why didn't we get any responses to the ad?"

"Beats me. Maybe folks don't want to call long distance."

I didn't like any of this. He sounded like a country and western singer ad-libbing a few lines between verses. The only fact he knew was that the ad had appeared in the newspaper, and it was possible that he had the name right. Dickie Foster's husband remembered Terry. Teddy wasn't a far cry from that, but it didn't mean this person was a brother. "Do you know any places Natalie worked in New York?" I asked.

"Yeah, there was an ad agency downtown somewhere. Hopkins and Something?"

"What about before that?"

"Before that?"

"Yes. She worked somewhere before she went to work for Hopkins." I wasn't going to give him a syllable, although he probably knew the full name of the company.

"You know, I don't remember just now. I'd have to go

back to her old letters and see if she mentioned a name. That's over five years ago."

"How did you know about Hopkins?"

"She wrote and said she got the job. Then I went away for a while and kinda lost track of her."

"Would you mind giving me the name and phone number of your parents?"

"Oh, Chris, I wish I could. They're long gone. I'm the only one left. Besides Natalie." The words kept rolling out, slippery with grease.

"Can you give me your phone number?"

"My phone number?" There was a small sound and then he said, "I'm kinda hard to reach. I'm borrowing a phone right now and I won't be here after today. But I tell you what. If I find out the name of that place she used to work for, I'll give you a ring, how's that?"

"Fine."

"And can you tell me how it is you're looking for my sister?"

"The people who know her want her found."

"How'd you get to Connersville?"

"Luck," I said.

"Well, I hope you keep havin' luck because mine ran out. I haven't seen my sister in over five years and I don't know what's happened to her or where she is. And since she's my only living relative, I'd like to find her."

"Keep looking," I said.

The phone call unnerved me. I restrained myself from calling the newspaper I had placed the ad in. If this man really had a friend there, the friend wouldn't be likely to admit having given out my name and phone number. What was certain was that "Ted" knew about the ad. So had the person who had called Sandy. Could they possibly be one and the same person? It seemed doubtful. Whoever had called Sandy had been threatening. This person had been on the verge of breaking into song.

He hadn't given me one smidgen of information, but he had pumped me for what I knew. In the end it had been a standoff, but he had my name and number and I didn't have his. And the likelihood was, he knew where I lived. Jack wouldn't be any happier about that than I was. My only comfort was that the streets here were empty overnight by law and any car parked on the street in daylight would be visible and raise questions. It was a lot easier to hide in the jumble of the city than in a quiet town.

23

Jack was concerned enough about my being followed on Wednesday morning that he scouted the area before I left and followed me several miles to where I picked up the highway. He was becoming distinctly unhappy about my involvement in this, his other persona emerging, the tough, morose one that saw the black side of life and wanted to keep it from encroaching on ours.

I worked my way west and north and picked up Route 17, passing old towns that had become familiar to me on earlier trips: Goshen, Monticello, Liberty, Roscoe, and my favorite, Fishs Eddy. There was new snow on the fields, but the road was clean as summer and I made good time to Binghamton, where I got off and followed the handwritten directions once again.

Although New York is such a populous state, I have often thought that you could drop a stranger into any number of parts of it and have him believe he was in the heartland of this country. There are miles of forest and fields, an abundance of tiny dwellings and great estates. What one sees nowadays rather ubiquitously is the satellite dish that carries television to areas outside the heavily populated metropolitan ones. As I passed one after the other, I found myself wishing there were a way to disguise them, to preserve the rustic nature of the land, but I guess it's too late for that. They give a high-tech look to what ought to be the lowest-tech-looking area of the state.

I stopped before the last leg and had some lunch, then, refreshed, continued. Before reaching the orchard, I noticed a car pulled off to the side of the road, apparently empty, a bad place, I thought, to run out of gas or develop car trouble. At the orchard, I slowed, turned, and bumped my way to Al DiMartino's half-hidden driveway.

His carport was empty, so I pulled over in the tracks I had made last week, noticing how fresh they still looked. There hadn't been any snow. I hoped it would hold off another few hours. I had no plans to spend a lot of time here, although I had brought an overnight bag along in case the weather made the return trip look difficult.

I got out of the car and walked around a little, hoping he would return quickly. He had to know I was on my way since he had left the message yesterday morning. But half an hour passed and he wasn't there. I didn't like the feeling of déjà vu, the memory of last week's ordeal before he let me in. It was just as cold this week and I wanted to get home tonight.

Forty-five minutes and still no sign of him. And then it struck me. The car I had passed before reaching the orchard. It could have been DiMartino's car. I am notoriously poor at recognizing automobiles. I am probably one of only a handful of Americans for whom a car is transportation, the cheaper and longer lasting the better. I don't even admit how old my own car is for fear of putting a jinx on it. But if that car had been his, he had had some trouble and might be almost anywhere looking for help.

I got in my car and backed into the garage, then pulled out forward and drove through the trees to the road. I kept my eyes peeled as I went, but there was no one either on foot or in a vehicle. At the crossroad, I turned right and drove past the orchard. I remembered I had spotted the car before I reached the orchard, and as I looked, I saw it, still off the road on my left. I made a U-turn and parked behind it, getting out to see if he had left any kind of note in the windshield.

There was no note, but there was someone inside stretched out on the front seat and it was Al. I caught my breath and told myself this was not the time to panic. The driver's door was unlocked and I opened it, saying, "Sergeant? Sergeant DiMartino?" as I leaned in.

"Chris," a whispered sound came. "Chris, Chris." He had been sitting behind the wheel when he had been stricken, probably with just enough time to pull off the road. Then he had lain or fallen to his right so that his head was near the passenger door. He said something, but I couldn't understand it.

"What?" I asked, knowing I should be getting help, not wasting time talking.

He said it again, then once more, and I realized he was saying "heart." He'd had a heart attack, or at least he thought so.

For a moment I felt utter confusion, not sure whether I should take my car to the orchard and call an ambulance, push DiMartino over and drive his car there, or drive him to a hospital myself. When I made a decision, it was more to get things moving than to do what was right.

"I'm taking you to the hospital," I said. "I'll help you move over and then I'll drive into town." I reached over while I was talking and unlocked the far door. Then I ran around to the other side, opened the door, and got him into the passenger seat with a lot of help from him. When he was sitting, I fastened the seat belt, let the back of his seat down just a little so he would incline backward, and then I ran back and got the car started.

Luckily, I ran into a policeman as I entered town and he not only directed me, he led me, lights and siren going, to the small hospital a few miles away. He must have radioed ahead because they were waiting for us and got DiMartino inside in record time.

Officer Tallman sat with me for a few minutes, getting details about DiMartino. I told him the sergeant was a retired policeman and I saw the subtle change. Officer Tallman was not just doing his duty; now he was helping one of his own.

"He has a wife or ex-wife somewhere," I said.

"I'll get hold of his wallet and have a look. You have any idea how long he was in that car before you found him?"

"No idea at all. I don't even know if it's since this morning or yesterday."

"Poor guy."

An aide came into the waiting room at that moment, saw me, and asked if I was Mrs. Brooks.

"I am. How is he?"

"It doesn't look good, but we have a fine cardiologist here and they're doing the best they can. He wants you to have his house keys. I couldn't quite understand what he was saying."

"I came to collect something he made for me."

"I'll drive you over," the cop said. "You can pick up your car on the way."

At the house I let us in. The place looked neater than last week, the bed made, the sink almost empty. He had worked at cleaning up for company. I felt terrible. This was a man with talent and energy, condemned to disgrace and a lonely life because a system he had loved and served well had been turned inside out to hurt him.

"He's an artist," the cop said, amazement in his voice. "I've never seen anything like this."

"He was a forensic sculptor for the New York Police Department. He did something for me." I turned to find Natalie and saw her near the woodstove. Next to her was a girl with a lopsided nose and a quirky face, Natalie in her late teens. I walked toward the sculptures holding my breath.

"Musta been in that car a long time," Officer Tallman said, his hand on the stove. "Stove's cold."

"Here she is."

"Who?"

"The woman I'm looking for twenty years ago."

"How'd he do that?"

"It's his genius. This is how she looked when she disappeared."

"Fantastic."

"Yes, really fantastic." A large envelope was propped against the older Natalie. Inside were several eight-by-ten black-and-white pictures of both sculptures. "He must have had these done yesterday," I said. I realized both heads had hair. Heaven only knew where DiMartino had found wigs, but a wig sat on each head, brown on the younger Natalie, auburn on the older one. They weren't real hair, but the pictures looked so lifelike, I knew they would do for our purposes.

"Here's a book of addresses," the cop said from the desk. "Loretta DiMartino? Sound like his wife?"

"Sounds like a relative anyway."

"I'll take it along."

I had brought a couple of boxes with me and some soft cloth to wrap the heads in. The officer carried one and I took the other out to my car. The pictures I had left with DiMartino last week were on the floor near the stand with one of the sculptures. I had a lot of money I wanted to give him, but I didn't want to leave it in an empty cabin. We drove back to the hospital.

Someone had already called his wife—she was still his wife, it seemed—and she was on her way. I asked a couple of times if I could see him, but they wouldn't let me. Everyone looked grim and I settled in to wait for his wife or for a chance to see DiMartino. I had brought a book with me in case I stayed over. Now I read it distractedly, my attention wandering at every movement, every sound. I wished I could have a few minutes to address the medical team, to tell them about the man they were working on, to let them know this was a worthy human being, a person who had devoted himself to public service, that he had accomplishments that would be remembered, artistic talent greater than that of most people, that if he had erred, he had already paid a heavy price and he deserved to live out his three score years and ten. I saw myself as his advocate, but I had no audience for my thoughts, only myself, and I was already convinced.

It was a long afternoon. When I knew I would not be able to make it home, I called and left a message for Jack, then called our own number and left the same message on our answering machine. From time to time a nurse would come out and update me, but there was little real news.

"We're still working on him," one of them said.

"Keep hoping," from the other.

At six a middle-aged woman in a gray coat and black boots stepped into the waiting room and looked around as though expecting someone to be waiting for her.

"Mrs. DiMartino?" I said, standing.

"Yes. I'm Loretta. Who are you?"

"Chris Bennett. I found your husband. I was coming to pick up some sculptures he did for me."

"Do you know where I can find the doctor?"

I took her to the nurses' station and they picked up from there. She was gone for a long time and I sat with my open book, wondering what effect her presence would have on DiMartino—if he was aware enough to know she was at his side. She came back to the waiting room finally, looking worn and miserable, and sat beside me.

"There's a lot of damage," she said in a low voice. "It would've been better if he'd gotten here right away. He was out in that freezing cold for hours."

"I passed his car on my way to the house, but I didn't know it was his car. I wish I'd stopped."

"It's not your fault, honey. If not for you, he'd still be out in the cold." She patted my hand and gave me a smile. "He's a crazy man, my Al. Never learned how to keep his mouth shut. I used to say, 'Al, do your work and mind your business,' and he'd say, 'Loretta, I can't stand by and watch them make mistakes. The Constitution gives me the right to say what I think.' But he was wrong. The Constitution doesn't give you any rights on the job. They should have read him the Miranda warnings when he got out of the Academy."

I smiled at her assessment. "I admire a man who says what he thinks," I said.

"So do I, but admiration doesn't pay the bills, and they were out to get Al so long, I knew they'd do it eventually. Why can't a man learn to live with his mouth shut? He loved his work. He could've been still doing it and getting a paycheck and living in a decent house with heat and three square meals a day."

"I only met him once, but he struck me as a good man."

"Better than good," she said under her breath. "Just raving mad. You don't have to stay, honey. I'm OK. Go home to your husband."

"Would you like to go to a motel for the night?"

"I can't leave."

"What did the doctor say?"

"He probably won't make it the night."

I went to the coffee shop and picked up some greasy hamburgers and worse coffee and brought them upstairs. We ate together, waiting for something to happen, hoping it would be good or, failing that, that nothing would happen, that he would get through the night unchanged and start to recover when the sun rose.

I fell asleep at one point, never one to stay awake easily

after dark. When I awoke sometime after midnight, Loretta was gone. I went to the ladies' room and washed, wishing I had my toothbrush from my overnight bag, but that was out in the car. I found a nurse in the hall who told me Loretta was with Al, so I went back to the waiting room and sat and closed my eyes again. I woke up with a start at two A.M. There was noise and activity, people running. I walked to where I could see them, but they disappeared around a corner and I didn't want to walk down the hall to see where they were going. Sometimes not knowing is a comfort.

At two-thirty Loretta reappeared. I didn't have to ask. It was in her face, her shoulders, the very fit of her skin.

"He's gone," she said.

I stood and went over to her, put my arm around her shoulders.

"The doctor said, 'We lost him,' and I said, 'What do you mean, you lost him? You never had him.' I had him, thirty-two years if you count the ones he lived in that shack. I'm the one that lost him. Goddamn job. It'll kill you every time."

"Let's go find a place to sleep, Loretta."

"Why not," she said.

We slept till after eight, sharing a room in the motel I had stayed in last week. I called Jack when I got up and told him the news. Then Loretta and I dressed and went down for breakfast. She was a thin woman who looked older than I thought she was, and she ate as if breakfast were not part of her daily activities. When we finished, we checked out and drove to the hospital. Loretta had left her car there. She dropped her bag in it and we went inside together. After a few formalities, she called a mortuary in Queens and they promised to drive out to pick up Al's body.

"It's done," she said as she put down the phone. "I'm glad you were here, but I'm OK now. You go home."

I protested, but she really meant it.

"I'm a cop's wife. I know the score."

"I can drive you back."

"And then figure out how to get my car back to Queens? I'm better off driving myself. Honest. You're a honey, Chris. Go home."

"Loretta, I never paid Al for his work." I opened my bag and took out my wallet. "We agreed on four hundred dollars."

"He charged you that?" Her voice rose in disbelief.

I took out the four hundreds I had gotten from the bank. "We agreed on that. It's yours now."

She took it and looked at it. "Thanks, honey," she said.

"He deserved it."

"That and a lot more. I wish it had come to him."

24

I was home by afternoon and I let Jack and Sandy know I had arrived. Sandy was anxious to see the sculpture of the young Natalie.

"You're welcome to come out and look," I said, feeling weary and hoping he wouldn't take me up on my invitation today, "but I'm going ahead with ads in Indiana and upstate New York right away."

"Don't you think I should see what you've got first?"

"Frankly, I don't, Sandy. I think what I've got is as close as we're going to come to what Natalie looked like twenty years ago, and whether you like what you see or not, it's all we've got. It's clear she has a Midwest connection and I think she has an upstate connection." I hadn't told him about Martin Jewell's weekend with Natalie, but he knew about Dickie Foster's postcard. "So I want to move ahead."

"All right, go ahead."

"I'm probably going to run over the five hundred dollars of expenses. I paid Al DiMartino's widow four hundred, and there'll be bills for ads and some other miscellaneous expenses."

"No problem. You're already way ahead of anyone else, as I'm sure I've told you."

"I've got the names of a couple of newspapers in Saratoga and Warren Counties. I'm going to hit them all."

"Sounds good."

I spent some time typing copy for the ads. Tomorrow

Jack would have copies made of the photographs and the copy, and he would send them out for me. When the envelopes were addressed, I fell into bed.

None of the ads made the Sunday paper. I was grateful for the hiatus. The trip to Al DiMartino's house and his struggle and death had left me tired and sad. The phone call from "Ted Miller" had left me looking over my shoulder. On Friday I took care of household chores, looking forward to having Jack home for dinner and the weekend. It would be nice to have some quiet in our lives, a little of that mythical togetherness I had heard about but not experienced very much. I called Joseph at St. Stephen's and briefed her. Then I told her, finally, about my search for the woman at the Thanksgiving Day parade.

"Why do you want to find her?" she asked.

"I'm not sure I can explain it. I feel somehow that she's part of my life."

"You're sure she's not a cousin or something of your father?"

"I'm not sure of anything. I just know that she knew my name, that she acted as though she belonged with us."

"But you're afraid your father was seeing her."

"I think it's possible," I said carefully.

"If she were a relative, can you think of a reason why your father wouldn't say, 'This is Cousin Isabel,' or 'This is Aunt Isabel'?"

"Not even a remote reason. But Jack and I both think my mother's old friend knows something she doesn't want to tell me."

"She'll tell you eventually, Chris. She'll want to get it off her chest."

"I hope so."

"Keep me posted on the Natalie case."

"I will."

* * *

Should I call Elsie Rivers? I took a walk in the afternoon and stopped at Melanie's for a cup of coffee. We talked for an hour about Natalie and what I had learned. In the warmth of her family room, I relaxed and enjoyed her company and her cookies. But the moment I stepped outside her house, I thought of Elsie again.

Her call last weekend had been strange. She had said we should get together, but she hadn't extended an invitation or suggested a date. In fact, the mention of a get-together had sounded more like an introduction to our conversation than a reason for calling. I knew that if I was wrong, if I had misinterpreted the call, I was heading for disappointment, but Jack had also thought there was something she wanted to say when we had visited her two weekends ago.

It turned out I could have saved myself the agonizing internal discourses I had been going through. Elsie called on Saturday afternoon.

"I was just thinking of you," I said, telling the truth with no embellishment.

"Well, I've been thinking of you, too, Chris, just sitting here with my knitting and thinking of Francie and you and how I'd really like to see you again."

"Would you like to come here for a visit?" I asked.

"No, I think I'd like you right here in my little house, and if your Jack doesn't mind, why don't you come on over by yourself? It'll be like Francie and me all those years ago."

"I'd love to. Shall we pick a time?"

"Why not Monday afternoon? Both our husbands'll be out of the house and we can have a little peace and quiet." She said it as though the husbands kept up a steady din in our respective houses.

"Monday is fine."

"Come at two. Two's a good time."

As good a time as any, I thought, accepting.

* * *

There was nothing to sit home for on Monday anyway. The Indiana paper promised to run the ad Tuesday through Sunday. One of the upstate New York papers came out only on Wednesday, and the daily said they would run the ad Tuesday through Sunday, like the Indiana paper. No one was running it on Monday.

I stopped at a local florist in Oakwood and picked up a few stems of baby orchids to give to Elsie. Then I drove over, parking in her driveway.

Her smile, as always, was spontaneous and genuine. She oohed over the flowers, then put them in a lovely little vase that seemed made for a spray of delicate flowers. She had tea on a warming plate and little square cakes coated with chocolate and topped with buttercream flowers on a crystal serving plate. We carried everything out to a glass-enclosed room at the rear of the house.

"What a lovely spot," I said, setting down the cakes.

"Francie would have loved it. We didn't build it till ten years ago. In the summer you can't even see through the trees, the leaves are so dense."

There were small silver cake forks that looked antique, and I remembered my mother talking about how Elsie liked to go to flea markets and shows and pick things up. To hear my mother tell it, Elsie made a killing every time, finding treasures in junk, underpriced items that were worth far more than the asking price, quality amidst trash.

"The forks are beautiful," I said.

"Had 'em for years. There were just five and she gave them to me for a song. What's so special about an even number? They're just great for the two of us and another couple. I don't entertain big crowds much anyway."

I had brought my wedding album for her to see and we turned the pages together. There was Sister Joseph, Sister Angela, my mother-in-law, Jack's sister, the chapel at St. Stephen's decorated for the occasion. Elsie was thrilled, asking about each person, trying to put them in the context of my life. Finally I closed the book and poured some more tea.

"You said something last time you were here, Kix. You don't mind if I call you Kix, do you?"

"I like it."

"You were such a good child. I hope you have one like yourself one day."

"Thank you. I hope so, too."

She was easily diverted, unwilling to go ahead with what she had planned in advance to tell me. "You talked about the parade."

"Yes. My dad took me."

"And you met someone there."

"A woman. I don't remember her name."

"I think your mother told me about her."

Prepared as I was for a revelation, her words hit me like a slap. My heart started pounding and a voice in my head told me I didn't want to hear it, I DIDN'T WANT TO HEAR IT. I looked at her, suddenly hoping she would change her mind and I could go home without knowing any more than I knew now.

"Your mom . . ."

"Yes?"

"I wasn't supposed to tell you. She didn't mean for me to know. She told me one day when she was feeling very low. Your mom had a sister, Kix."

I shook my head. My mother was an only child. I had been to my grandparents' house when I was young and I had seen their pictures and there was only Frances. She had always said she was an only child.

"It's true, dear. There was a sister. She did things she shouldn't have. They disowned her, your grandparents. And your mother went along with it."

"But why?"

"Bad things," Elsie said. "She hurt her parents, hurt them a lot. Your mom told me."

"I don't understand. You think she's the one we talked to on Thanksgiving Day?"

"Oh, I know it. Francie told me once after you and your dad saw her. Your dad always wanted to get them together. He was a real peacemaker."

I started to cry. It was all so crazy. Here I was, dealing with people like Al DiMartino, who couldn't keep his family together, and Natalie Gordon, who had segmented her life and left a great chasm between the two parts so they would never meet, and in my own family a similar craziness had existed, a craziness my wonderful father had tried and failed to extinguish.

"It's all right, honey," Elsie said with dismay. "These things happen in every family. I just didn't want you to think, God forbid, that your wonderful father was meeting some woman behind your mother's back. It was your own aunt, Chris. She was your own flesh and blood."

I took the tissue she pressed into my hand and cleaned up my face. "Thank you, Elsie. Thank you for telling me."

She put another cake on my plate, as though I were a hurt child who would be comforted by the sweet taste of sugar and chocolate. My emotions were going so crazy, I couldn't tell whether I felt more relieved that my father was a hero or shocked that my mother had severed relations with her own sister.

"I wonder if she's still alive," I said finally.

"Why not? Your own mother'd only be in her fifties if she was around today."

"Do you know her name?"

"I think Francie said Olive. That doesn't ring a bell, does it?"

I shook my head. If they had talked about her, it had been when I wasn't around.

"You think you'll call her?"

"I'll try to find her. Was she married?"

"That's part of it," Elsie said, looking troubled. "But I

don't think she used her married name. I think she kept her maiden name, at least when your mother was alive."

I didn't want to ask for any of the sordid details, and it didn't look like Elsie wanted to reveal them. I put myself back together and split the last cake with her—I think she wanted it more than I did—and then left, feeling overchocolated and still overwrought.

At home I pulled out the Manhattan directory that we kept in the house and looked up my mother's maiden name, Cleaver. There were several, none with the first name Olive, but there was an O. A. Cleaver on West Sixty-fourth Street, exactly where I had expected to find her. With pounding heart, I dialed the number, but there was no answer.

Tomorrow I would find out once and for all.

25

The prospect of finding what was surely my last living blood relative besides my cousin Gene so consumed me that I lost all interest in staying home to await calls from Sandy Gordon. I had to get to New York and see if my aunt was in the apartment on Sixty-fourth Street, and I couldn't wait. After I taught my class, I grabbed a very quick lunch in the cafeteria and drove directly to the city.

I found her name next to a button in the lobby and pressed it, waiting impatiently, keyed up, for any kind of response. None came. I rang again, feeling increasingly disheartened. She was at work, she was away on vacation, she was somewhere she would rather be and might not be back for a long time.

The lobby door opened and a well-dressed woman stepped out.

"Excuse me, do you know Miss Cleaver in 2B?" I asked.

"I don't think so. I live higher up. The super should be around somewhere. Maybe he can help you." She left without waiting for me to say anything, and I turned back to the list of names, finding SUPER at the last bell. I rang it.

A woman in jeans and a sweatshirt and carrying a young child opened the door. "You ring for the super?"

"Yes. I'm looking for Miss Cleaver in 2B."

"She's not there."

"Do you know where she is?"

"They took her away to the hospital again. Last week sometime."

"Do you know which hospital?"

She shrugged. "Same one as before, I guess."

It didn't look as though I was talking to a good or willing source of information. "Would you have any idea how I could find her?"

"You could leave a note in her mailbox or with me. If I see her, I'll give it to her."

That didn't sound like a productive move. "Thank you," I said. "I'll see if I can find the hospital."

"Sure," she said indifferently, and pushed open the door she had been holding off the latch.

I went outside, turned toward Broadway, and found a store that let me see a phone book. Roosevelt Hospital was only half a dozen blocks away, a likely place to be taken if you're picked up by ambulance. I called and asked if Olive Cleaver was a patient.

"Yes, she is," a Spanish-accented voice said. "You wanna be connected?"

"No, thank you. Are visiting hours in effect now?"

"Yes, ma'am."

I walked down and found the hospital. A pleasant woman checked her computer and found Olive Cleaver. They gave me a pass to insure that there would be no more than two visitors at one time. Clutching the pass like a child holding her mother's hand in a hostile area, I made my way through the maze of corridors and elevators to the room where my aunt lay.

Most of the doors I passed were open, so I slowed as I approached hers, trying to calm myself, wondering what I would say, whether she would want to see me, how we would make up for a lifetime of being apart. I stopped just short of the room. That door, too, was open, an invitation to enter. Swallowing, I turned and went inside.

The first bed was occupied by a tiny sleeping figure, an

ancient woman with thin white hair and hands that moved as she slept, as though she were shooing away flies or bad dreams. Between her bed and the next a curtain was drawn. I walked to it, looked around it, and set foot on Olive Cleaver's territory.

"Olive?" I asked.

She was thin, maybe in her sixties but looking older, washed-out blond-gray hair too long to be kept in place on a pillow, skin so pale it might never have seen the light of summer. She turned from the window and fixed her gray eyes on me, holding them there, putting together all her memories, maybe even all her hopes and dreams.

"You're her daughter," she said.

I tried desperately not to cry. "I'm Christine."

"I remember. Pull up a chair. How did you find me?"

I took the guest chair and sat between the bed and the window. "I remembered you at the Thanksgiving Day parade."

She smiled a little, or at least her lips did. "I used to meet you and Eddie there. Then one year he didn't come."

"He died." I could hardly speak, but she seemed totally unaffected, completely without emotion.

"She never told me." There was a harshness to her voice. Her sister had disappointed her.

"My mother died seventeen years ago."

"I'm sorry to hear that."

"It was very hard for her after Dad died."

"What did you do? You couldn't have been very old."

"I went to live with my aunt Meg, Dad's sister."

"Eddie was a good man." She said it as though he had cared for me, not his sister.

"And when I was fifteen, I went to live in a convent. I became a nun."

She closed her eyes and shook her head. "Is that what Francie wanted for you?"

"I think so. It was what I wanted for myself. I left almost two years ago. I'm married now."

"Seems to be the way the world is going." She pulled herself up so she was more sitting than lying, holding a hand up to keep me from helping her. "Did she leave you my name and address?"

I shook my head. "I talked to my mother's friend. She knew about you. It took a while, but she told me yesterday. I guessed you lived in this area because we used to meet you on the street with the Statue of Liberty."

She closed her eyes and nodded. "Kids remember things. I've lived here a long time."

"Elsie—my mother's friend—said there were problems between you and your parents."

"Lots of problems. Big problems. I was a bad girl." She said it almost with a touch of pride, as though she had ventured to do things her generation could not approve of.

"I'm sure they couldn't have been that bad."

"They were."

"I guess you're here because you're sick," I said, not wanting to pry.

"Very sick. It's all catching up with me now. But I'll be going home soon, maybe in a day or two."

"That's wonderful."

"Not so wonderful. They can't do much more for me. I don't want to die in a hospital. I hate it here. I have a nice apartment. That's where I belong."

"Would you like to come to our house?"

"No. You're a nice girl, Christine. You don't want me there and I don't want to be there. It's too bad about Eddie. He never told you about me, did he?"

"No one did. I just remembered you and wanted to know who you were."

"Your mom wouldn't like this, you know. She didn't want us to meet. I'm a bad influence on young girls." She laughed and it ended in a cough that left her breathing with difficulty.

"Have you seen a priest?" I asked.

"Not for a long time. There's nothing a priest can do for me. I did bad things and I hurt people. I stole from my parents."

"Why?"

"I needed the money. Or at least I thought I did. I was pregnant."

"They would've helped you."

"No. No they wouldn't. It was a different time, forty years ago. They were people who knew what was right. They're hard to deal with, people like that. I think Francie could've forgiven me almost anything except the money, and she was right. I kept thinking I would pay them back someday, but they hated me too much. I couldn't do it. I never saw them again. Francie and I tried to work something out, but we couldn't. Then Eddie tried. Eddie the peacemaker. Your mother married a good man, I'll say that for her."

"Did you have an abortion?"

"Not that time. The first time I gave her up for adoption. It was for the best. I couldn't take care of a baby. She never came looking for me and I never went looking for her. That's the best way." She took a breath and lay back, closing her eyes.

"Can I get you anything?" I asked.

She shook her head.

"Olive, I want to see you again."

She turned her head back and forth on the pillow. "Just leave your name and number so someone can call you when I die. You'll hear in a week or two. I don't have much time left."

"I'll come to see you. If you're feeling better, maybe we can take a walk together."

"Your daddy's girl," she said. "I remember you at the parades, all dressed up. Those were such nice parades. I would've watched them even if Eddie hadn't brought you." She closed her eyes again and I watched her breathe deeply. She was asleep.

I stayed for a few minutes, but she didn't wake up. I stood, touched her forehead with my hand, and then bent and kissed it. Then I left.

I called Sandy when I got home.

"No calls," he said curtly. "Nothing. Nothing's going to happen this time."

"It's early," I said. "Lots of people don't even look at the paper till they get home at night. Don't forget to forward your calls tonight."

"I won't." There was an almost surly overtone to his voice, something totally out of character. He always struck me as such a mild, easygoing man. It was getting to him finally.

"Tomorrow's the day," I said. "It'll be in more papers tomorrow. You'll hear something."

"I'll let you know."

Jack and I talked about Olive in bed that night with the lights out. "She's dying," I said. "She's so matter-of-fact about it, it's shocking. 'Give me your name and phone number so they can call you when I die. It'll be a week or so.'"

"She's probably had a long time to accept it."

"I can't bear the thought of her dying alone."

"I think you have to respect her wishes, Chris. Just because she wants something different from what you would want, she sounds like a woman who knows her own mind."

"She is."

"You want her to forgive your mother, don't you?"

In the dark, I wiped away the tears. My mother was perfect. I loved her without reservation, without if clauses and then clauses. I admired her life, her struggle, her relentless optimism in the face of disaster. If there were flaws in me, they were of my own making. "I guess so," I said, as usual, surprised that my husband read me so well.

"Don't expect miracles. Offer, but don't be surprised if she turns you down."

I knew it was good advice. "She looks like my mother. I don't think I ever saw it when I was a child. Maybe it's my grandmother she looks like. The age is about the same. She must have been a pretty girl."

"She say how much money was involved?"

"No, but it must have been substantial for my grandparents to disown her."

"You found her, honey. It's enough."

"It's funny, all this talk about Natalie's brother who wasn't supposed to exist. I think I knew she was going to be a sibling. I think I expected it."

"I love you, baby."

I turned to him with an equal love, and accepted his arms.

26

Wednesday morning I called the hospital and talked to Olive briefly. She was tired and didn't want company. She expected to be sent home Thursday or Friday, as soon as arrangements could be made for home assistance. I made some offers and she turned them down, but she gave me her home phone number, which I hadn't asked for, and I promised to keep in touch.

I worked at my poetry class, finishing everything that needed to be done for next week. During the hours I sat at my desk, the phone never rang. I didn't know what time of day the weekly paper came out upstate, but I felt edgy. It was going to happen soon, someone recognizing the picture of Al DiMartino's sculpture.

Finally, finished with my classwork, I put my coat on, made sure the answering machine was on, and left the house. The sun was shining so brightly, it felt warm. I stuck my hands in my pockets and walked through a couple of streets to the strip of beach we all owned equally, a cove on Long Island Sound owned by a community organization Aunt Meg had always been part of. I stepped on the sand and it was again like Proust with his madeleines dipped in tea. I remembered coming here early in my relationship with Jack, walking along this strip with the first man in my life, feeling sensations I had never felt before or that I had repressed. There was a cold wind from the water today, but it made me feel good. I love the smell of the sea, and the sound is almost the Atlantic Ocean. I walked the half-moon strip, reliving happy memories. Someday, I hoped, I would take a child of mine to feel the water lapping on the beach.

The beach was empty today. Aunt Meg used to joke on summer days when one other person was there that it was crowded. Today I was the crowd. I walked around the cove to the end, then turned and came back again, feeling refreshed. Then I went home.

It was late afternoon now. Sandy would be leaving for home soon, or perhaps to work out at a gym or take in a movie. I picked up the phone and called him.

"Hello?" He was still answering the line himself.

"It's Chris. Has anything happened?"

"Very little. I've come to a decision, Chris. I was going to call you when I got home. I want to end our investigation."

"What do you mean?" I was aghast. It was impossible to stop now.

"Just what I said. It's over. Send me a bill for whatever expenses my initial five hundred hasn't covered and let's call it a day."

"Sandy, what's happened?"

"Nothing's happened. Nothing's going to happen. Natalie is gone. I'll never see her again. I've had a long time to get used to it. I think the time has come to get on with my life, as they say. I want to meet new women, get back in the swing of things."

"Sandy, something's happened that you haven't told me."

"What has happened is that I've had a change of heart."

"I have to tell you, if you drop this, I intend to turn over everything I've learned to the detective in charge of the police investigation."

There was a pause. Then he said, "Do what you have to. It's over." Then he hung up.

It wasn't over for me. There was no doubt in my mind he had gotten a phone call with some kind of information he couldn't handle and he didn't want to go any further. But I had to. Natalie Gordon was a real person who had disappeared, and whether she was alive or dead, I had to find out the truth. I got my notebook and looked up the numbers of the upstate New York newspapers. I called the daily first and asked for the advertising department.

"I put an ad in your paper to run from yesterday through the weekend. My name is Christine Bennett."

"Oh yes," a girlish voice said. "The pictures of the woman."

"That's the one. Have you had any calls about it?"

"Not that I know of. Didn't you have a telephone number in the ad?"

"I did, but I wondered whether anyone had called you with questions or information."

"I don't think so. Let me check my desk." She moved papers around and then came back. "I don't think so, Ms. Bennett."

I thanked her and called the weekly.

"You know what?" a youngish male voice said when I asked my question. "Someone here on the paper recognized one of those pictures."

"Really?"

"Yeah. He got pretty excited about it. Said he remembered her well."

"Do you know who it was?"

"One of the big editors. Can you hold on?"

"Sure."

He put me on hold and my spirits rose. I could hardly contain my excitement. I was practically counting seconds when a voice said, "Roger Belasco."

"Mr. Belasco, this is Christine Bennett. I understand you recognized a picture I ran in your paper, a woman I'm looking for."

"Oh yes, right. You got the name wrong and the hair's a little off, but I'd recognize that face anywhere. There was no mistaking that nose. I think her father broke it. It was a sad situation. I went to high school with her about a hundred years ago."

"What name do you remember her by?"

"That's Connie Moffat. Lived down the road from us. I think she left town after high school."

"Does she have any relatives left in town? Any old boy-friends? Girlfriends?"

"Well, the people who brought her up moved away, although I think they may have kept the old house as a summer place. There are probably plenty of guys who remember her, girls, too. They're women now, of course. A lot of our class stayed on in the area."

"Do you know where the family is?"

"I can probably find out. Want to give me your number?"

I recited it.

"What's happened? She run away or something?"

"She disappeared. It happened the Thanksgiving before last at Macy's parade."

"So if she was kidnapped, I guess you've got a million suspects, most of them under the age of ten."

"That's the way it looks."

"Ms. Bennett, if I cooperate with you, will you give us an exclusive on the story? If you find her, is it ours first?"

"Absolutely."

"I'll get back to you."

He called back in the evening, after I'd eaten dinner. The family that had taken Connie in after her parents died were cousins named Lewellyn. They had moved to Albany some years ago, but the old house was still owned by them, and Mrs. Lewellyn came out in the summer pretty regularly. He gave me a number.

"Were you in Connie's class?" I asked.

"Maybe a year ahead of her."

"May I ask you how old you are?"

"Forty-two on my next birthday."

"Thank you, Mr. Belasco. I can't tell you how helpful you've been."

"Just don't forget our agreement."

"Don't worry. You'll hear from me."

I called the number in Albany and a woman answered.

"Mrs. Lewellyn?"

"Yes." It was a sweet voice with a questioning tone.

"My name is Christine Bennett. I've been looking for Connie Moffat."

"Oh yes, Connie. Are you a friend of hers?"

"Not exactly. Do you know where she is?"

"I haven't seen or heard from her in years."

"Do you know how many?"

"Oh, quite a few. Three, four, five maybe."

"Could I come up and talk to you, Mrs. Lewellyn?"

"I wouldn't mind. I don't know what I can tell you."

"If I pick you up in Albany, could you direct me to your summer house?"

"I can take you there, but the heat isn't turned on. It's pretty cold."

"I just want to see it. Are you free tomorrow?"

"Let me see." She sounded like an older woman, a voice that had had years of use, concern in every syllable. "I have some things I have to do in the morning."

"I couldn't get there before eleven-thirty."

"Eleven-thirty's fine. It'll take another hour or so to get there."

"I'll bring lunch."

It would be painful, but I knew I had to talk to Sandy. He didn't answer his phone at first, allowing the machine to take over. But when he heard my name, he picked up.

"I talked to Roger Belasco," I said.

"I see."

"Sandy, whoever she was, she was your wife and she loved you."

"I know that. I'm just finding all this very difficult to accept. Belasco called this afternoon, and what he told me has left me pretty shaken. I already know more than I want to know, and I don't want any more revelations. I have certain memories and feelings that I'd like to preserve, so you'll have to understand if I decline to participate in any further investigation."

"I do understand. But I'm part of this now. I can't set it aside and pretend it's over."

"You do what you have to, Chris. I have a lot of thinking to do."

I knew it wouldn't help, but I said it anyway. "Don't think, Sandy. Just remember. For a time in your life, you had something very nice, both of you."

"Sure," he said, and I was dismissed.

I left after breakfast and took the Thruway, no scenic routes for me today. Today was business, business at my own expense since Sandy had removed himself from the search. It was easy to see why he was upset. He had been taken in and he was hurt and embarrassed, afraid to find out what other secrets his second wife had kept from him.

But there was another possibility that now occurred to me, a more sinister one, one I didn't want to entertain but had to, that in spite of what he had said last night, he had learned some or all of this while he was married to Natalie, that he himself had done away with her when he discovered the truth, that the truth I was about to uncover might point to him as a killer.

Mrs. Lewellyn's directions from the Thruway exit were clear and easy to follow. At twenty to twelve, I drove up her driveway. She came to the door with a smile. I went up the path and introduced myself, shaking her hand. She asked me in, but this wasn't the time for being sociable.

Ten minutes later we were on the road.

I explained as we drove. She hadn't seen any of the papers I had advertised in, so everything I said was new.

"You mean Connie's married?" she said, when I told her about Sandy.

"She married a very nice man about two years ago."

"Well, isn't that nice. She deserved a few good breaks, poor thing."

"I understand you brought her up."

"After her mother died. Her father left the family, and the mother died a year or so later. We're cousins, the Lewellyns and the Moffats. She was a skinny thing with clothes that didn't fit and an attitude you wouldn't believe. She was a handful, I'll tell you."

"How long did she live with you?"

"Till about the day she graduated from high school." She laughed.

"And then she took off?"

"Like a bat out of hell, my husband used to say."

"This house we're going to, is that where she lived?"

"All the time she was with us. I can even show you her old room, but it's a lot changed since then."

"Tell me about the last time you saw her."

"Oh my." She thought about it as though she were going through a mental calendar, trying to fit it into the chronology of her life. "Well, it's a few years ago, let me put it that way. I was sleeping upstairs and something woke me up. I went to the window and saw something moving downstairs. I went and got my husband's old shotgun and went down in my nightie. I opened the back door, the door to the garden, and there she was."

"What was she doing?"

"Just kinda standing there. I said, 'Connie, my goodness, why didn't you tell me you were coming?' and she said, 'I didn't know I was till I got here.' You know, that must have been the year of the tulip disaster, and that was about five years ago, I think. Or maybe it was after that, the next spring. Well, four or five years, I can't be sure."

"Did she say anything about herself, what she was doing?"

"She said she had a good job in New York, but she wouldn't give me an address. Said she just wanted to see the old place again. I never took Connie for sentimental, but you never know about people, do you?"

"It was night when she came?"

"It was dark. I don't recall if I looked at the clock."

That had to be when she and Martin Jewell spent a weekend together upstate. She had taken his car while he slept and driven up to the house for old times' sake. "Did you ever see her around Thanksgiving?" I asked.

"Never. Not since she left. I'm not usually at the house that late in the year anyway. It's too cold."

We kept up the chatter till we reached the house. Mrs. Lewellyn had a lot of memories she was happy to talk about. Connie had had a simply awful childhood, till she came to live with the Lewellyns, that is. Poor little thing once had her nose broken when she sassed her daddy. Her mother wasn't much good either and left nothing but debts when she died.

"Did Connie ever go to Indiana that you know about?"

"Not when she was living with us. I don't know what she's done since. We kept up a little after she went to New York, got a Christmas card most years, and then it stopped. I thought once she was going to get married—that must've been almost twenty years ago—and for all I know, she did, but she never told us. There's your turnoff just up ahead."

The conversation ended there and I concentrated on getting us where we were going. It was a pretty house set far enough back from the road so you could hardly see it till you reached the end of the drive. There were lots of tall evergreens as well as bare deciduous trees and shrubs, and the house itself looked very old. I asked her about it as I turned off the motor.

"Oh yes, it goes way back. Early eighteen hundreds, is what we've been told. That's why I hate to give it up. The kids love it, too, so one of them'll probably take charge of it. I just hope they keep up with the flowers."

We got out and she led the way to the front door. Inside it was almost as cold as out, and she had warned me in advance that the water was turned off to keep the pipes from freezing, so we couldn't use the sink or toilet. We had eaten on the way and stopped to wash before we got here.

I was quite charmed by the house. There were old timbers along the living room ceiling, and the well-cared-for floors were uneven in a way that indicated age. The kitchen had been carefully modernized, leaving old beams bare with kettles hanging from them.

I followed her up the steep, narrow stairs to the second floor, where there were four bedrooms, the last and smallest having belonged to Connie. There was a big oval rag rug on the floor and what looked like a handmade quilt on the bed, a lovely room for a single person. There wasn't much in it that would tell me anything about Connie because it had been occupied by other people in the decades since she had left. Down the hall was the bathroom, an ancient claw-foot tub surrounded by a plastic shower curtain prominent against the wall.

"Years ago I decided we should get a new tub," Mrs. Lewellyn said, "but my friend started telling me that the old claw-foot ones fetched a fortune now, so I left it. Makes it look awful old, though, doesn't it?"

"It looks lovely. I think this is a wonderful house."

"Well, I don't know what else I can tell you."

"Where did you see Connie that last time when she came at night?"

"Down back. I'll show you."

She held on to the banister going down, her feet side-

ways on the narrow treads, and I followed suit. She took
me to a back door that she opened with a key. We stepped
outside onto a concrete patio that was cracked with age.

"She was over there near that tree, the big oak at the
edge of the grass. I saw her from up there." She stepped
away from the house and pointed up.

I walked across the patio, then over to the tree. Any of
the windows on the back of the house would have a view
of this tree, and probably most of the lawn between the tree
and the patio. I went back, circling what looked like a
moss-covered flower bed.

"That's the tulips," she said as I neared. "I got a whole
bucket of bulbs one fall and planted 'em till my knees hurt.
Then the damn squirrels came and tossed them around the
place. I was madder'n hell," she said, using language I
hadn't expected from her. "My knees'll never forgive 'em."

"And you're not sure when that was."

"It's gotta be three or four years ago."

"Did you replant the tulips?"

"I did, and we put a netting over the place to keep the
squirrels away. It worked. You should see those tulips in the
spring." She looked cold, although the day was mild.

"Why don't we go somewhere for a cup of hot coffee?"
I suggested. "Then we can go back to Albany."

"That's all? You're finished here?"

"I'm finished," I said. I didn't want to tell her that I was
only starting.

27

"I think we have to try it, Jack."

It was the same night. I had come home late, worn out from a day at the wheel. "I think Connie or Natalie or whatever her name was hid something there, maybe when she sent the postcard to Dickie Foster. There are still two small keys on the ring. Maybe she buried a lockbox or suitcase. She came back a year later, or sometime later, I'm not exactly sure when, to make sure her secret was still intact. Whatever it is, it's going to answer all the questions we have."

"Let's go up on Saturday."

After I checked with Mrs. Lewellyn, I let Roger Belasco at the weekly newspaper know. She wasn't happy at the prospect of having her beautiful tulips dug up a second time, but I promised I would pay to have a gardener replant her bulbs, or new ones if she chose.

We got up at six on Saturday and drove up to Albany to pick her up. She was ready and we wasted no time setting out for the country house. We had a pickax and shovels in the trunk, but we needn't have bothered. Mrs. Lewellyn's garage had a great assortment of tools. At eleven-thirty, with a representative of the newspaper looking on, we set to work.

I have to admit my heart broke every time a bulb was unearthed. Some of them were already showing fresh spring shoots, and Mrs. Lewellyn took each one fondly, wrapped it, and put it in a box in the garage. The recent weather had not been cold enough to freeze the ground solid, and once we were through the top layer, the earth wasn't very hard to move. Not that it was easy, because it wasn't. We stopped to eat at Jack's suggestion (cops are always hungry), stopped to rest, stopped to chat with the newspaperman, whose name was Joe Belasco, Roger's son. Eventually young Joe, either embarrassed at watching Jack and me work or bored with doing nothing, picked up a shovel of his own and joined in.

He was the one who called, "Hold it," sometime after we had gotten back to work after breaking for lunch.

"What is it?" Jack and I said almost in chorus.

"Hit something. Maybe a rock, but there haven't been any rocks for a while."

"OK," Jack said. "Let's just take a look." He was all cop now, his voice a monotone, all business. He bent down where Joe pointed with the shovel and started pulling the earth away with his gloved hand as I knelt and watched. "Here we go. It's not a rock. It's—" He pulled some more earth. "Looks like a bone of some kind. Maybe a rib."

"What?" Joe said, paling.

I said nothing, but my stomach didn't like it.

"Looks like we've got a skeleton here, folks. I think this is the point when we stop working and call in the police."

They came pretty quickly, two young men who looked strong enough to wield shovels. They were also pretty excited, never having experienced anything like uncovering human remains.

Mrs. Lewellyn wept when I told her and refused to come outside. We had built a fire in the woodstove in the living room, and the downstairs was now comfortable enough to walk around in without a coat on. She remained in her chair, determined not to view whatever was being uncovered in her tulip bed. I went out and watched the careful, slower progress being made by the two uniformed officers under Jack's guidance. The bones were no longer held together, but I could see unpolished fingernails at the ends of fingers, buttons, teeth, a ratty-looking belt with a metal buckle.

"Hey, look at this," one of the officers said, leaning over the hole, which was now about three feet deep. He reached down and pulled out a woman's handbag.

It was dirty and wet, most likely black before the earth and weather attacked the color. The cop held it out and I walked over and took it from him. "Do you mind if I open it?" I asked.

"Go ahead. We need to know who it is. I guess it's a woman, right?"

I took it from him and went over to the patio table with Jack. I had to carry it with my hand at the bottom because the seams were coming apart. On the table, we got it open without tearing it, and I looked inside, then reached in. A wallet came out first, the kind with a purse to hold coins and several pockets for bills and cards. The first plastic card I pulled out had a name on it.

"Natalie Miller," I said.

"Not Gordon?"

"Miller," I repeated. "And here's a Social Security card. She must have had it laminated. It's in perfect shape. Natalie Miller."

"Keep looking."

And then I found it, a New York State driver's license issued to Natalie Miller, a color picture in the corner. The birth date made her about thirty-four now, and the face was one I had never seen a picture of. I took it inside and showed it to Mrs. Lewellyn. "Is that Connie?" I asked.

She barely glanced at it. "Not in a thousand years. Is this the girl who's buried in my garden?"

"I think so. It'll take a while to find out for sure, but it's a pretty safe bet it is."

"How'd she get there?"

"I'm not sure," I said, reluctant to answer with what I believed to be the truth.

"You think Connie killed her?"

"I think there's a very good chance."

"Lord in heaven."

"Can someone explain to me what's going on?" Joey Belasco was waiting for me as I came outside, notebook and pen in hand.

"I'll try," I said.

"I thought we were looking for Connie Moffat."

"We were, sort of."

"And whose body is this?"

"A woman named Natalie Miller."

"How'd she get here?"

"Probably she was murdered and buried here about five years ago."

"You think Connie did it?"

"I think it's likely." One of the policemen had told us a few minutes earlier that the skull appeared to have been bashed in, probably by a shovel, making everyone very uncomfortable about Mrs. Lewellyn's tools.

"So what's happened to Connie?"

"I think she's probably dead."

"You know where she is?" He held his pen up, waiting for me to speak.

"No, I don't. But I'm pretty sure I know who killed her."

"I have made so many stupid mistakes, Jack, I just can't believe what I've done."

"Enough," he said. "It's only one mistake."

"But I did it over and over."

"Don't tell me how dumb you are, OK? You found her. Nobody else even came close. Man, am I hungry."

We had driven Mrs. Lewellyn back to her Albany house and then we'd gotten ourselves a room at an inn out of town. It was too late to drive home and we both ached from digging, so we were making a night of it. I was hungry, too, starving, in fact, and we had to hurry down before the restaurant closed. But I was furious at my mistake, repeated over and over, or at least a couple of times. And much as I was now looking forward to dinner and a night with Jack in a romantic inn, I was anxious to get back to New York and clean up the case of Sandy Gordon's missing wife. But that would have to wait for tomorrow.

We drove straight to Manhattan when we left the inn on Sunday morning, and continued down to Gramercy Park. In front of Natalie's old apartment house, Jack sat at the wheel and I got out. Coming down the street was Dickie Foster, children and husband in tow.

"You looking for me?" she called.

"Yes. Hi. Hi, Mr. Foster. Nice to meet you. I'm Chris Bennett. Do you have a minute to look at a picture?"

"Sure. We've just been walking around, it's such a nice day."

I took out a copy of the picture of Connie Moffat, aka Natalie Gordon, and handed it to her. "Do you recognize her?"

"I think so. Paul, look at this." They put their heads together for a moment. Then Dickie said, "I think this was the girl who roomed with Natalie at the end, before she moved out."

"Then this isn't Natalie."

"Oh no. Natalie's small and blondish, nothing like this. This was a taller woman. I never met her; at least I don't remember her name."

"This is the woman I've been looking for," I admitted.

"But you said you were looking for Natalie."

"I think the woman in this picture killed Natalie and took over her identity. I never realized there were two missing women. You and I were talking about different people. I never showed you the picture or I would have known a long time ago what was going on."

"What a story. What do you think happened?"

"I think this woman killed Natalie around the time of the move. I'd guess Natalie had no intention of moving, but when she got killed, the killer had to go somewhere else to establish her new identity."

"Who would kill a nice girl like Natalie?"

"Maybe someone who wanted a good job and didn't have the credentials for it."

"I think we should move out of this city," Dickie said.

"Next year," her husband said. "I promise."

We drove home. Now I knew exactly when and where the transformation had taken place and I had a motive. There might have been more to it than that, an argument, a temper not well controlled, maybe some promises given and then broken. I might never find out, but there was still a chance Connie's killer knew, and I hoped he would tell me.

When we got home I went through my notes and then looked up a phone number. We had decided Jack would make the call while I listened on the upstairs phone.

It rang twice and then a familiar voice answered with, "Hi there."

"Hi yourself," Jack said in a bantering voice. "This Ted?"

There was silence. Then a far less happy voice said, "Who's this?"

Jack and I hung up. I had hit pay dirt.

* * *

Jack tracked down Detective Evelyn Hogan at her home and told her he had information on the disappearance of Natalie Gordon. Then I got on the phone and we agreed to meet the next morning at her office at One Police Plaza.

She was a nice-looking woman in her late thirties, dressed smartly in a gray suit with a white, collarless blouse, more, I thought, like a woman going to work in industry than a police detective.

"Nice to meet you, Mrs. Brooks," she said. "I'm Evelyn."

"I'm Chris, Chris Bennett most of the time."

"I hear you succeeded where I tried and failed."

"You didn't fail. You were right as far as you went. I had a lot of time, some very special help, and a lot of luck." I thought fleetingly of Sergeant Al DiMartino. "I think I know who kidnapped the woman known as Natalie Gordon, but I don't know what he did with her."

"I'm all ears. Can I get you some coffee?"

"Sure. Black."

We talked for some time and I let her Xerox my notes. She was impressed that I'd found the building near Gramercy Park and also that I had dug into the people at Hopkins and Jewell. Her predecessor on the case had made a few phone calls and listed them on the D.D. 5s but had never gone down to see anyone in person.

"So this is the one," she said when we reached the point in my notes where his name was.

"This is the one. It has to be."

"Let's give it a try." She picked up the phone, dialed, and asked for our suspect. "I see," she said, doodling on a piece of paper on her desk. "When was that? . . . Uh-huh. Any forwarding address? . . . OK. Thanks for your help." She hung up. "He quit. Didn't come in one day and they haven't seen him since. We'll have to stake out his apartment. You have that address?"

I had found it in the Brooklyn phone book yesterday and written it down.

"I'm not calling till we have manpower in place," Evelyn said. "I don't want to alert him that we're on to him. That call your husband made yesterday must have scared him. I hope it didn't scare him into leaving."

"So do I."

"We'll have to get a photo and put out a Want for Questioning, do some digging into his background, former employers, that kind of thing."

"I wonder what he's doing since he left Hopkins and Jewell."

"I'd guess he's found himself another job. It's pretty hard to live in New York without work. I'll get the Brooklyn Borough Detective Task Force in on it and assume we'll make our move when he gets home tonight. You're sure he has no idea you went upstate over the weekend and found that skeleton?"

"I'm sure. And it won't be published till Wednesday. It's a weekly that covered it."

"But there are police records now, and papers pick up that kind of story. I'm going to get the task force moving right away, in case he's home and tries to make a getaway. Can you identify him for us?"

"Absolutely."

"Now I've got to ask you some questions, and your answers are very important. I need more than a strong suspicion that this man, Theodore Miller, or whatever name he's using, is a killer."

"Before we go on," I said, interrupting her, "I'm a little confused. The body we dug up over the weekend isn't the body of Connie Moffat. How are you going to build a case against Ted Miller if we don't have a body?"

"It's tougher without a body, but it's been done before and we can do it this time if we have enough evidence, or a corroborative statement from someone who may have witnessed the killing or who Miller may have told about it, maybe with some incriminating details. At this moment I don't have a case. What I need from you is enough evidence that I can bring him in for questioning and search his apartment. So tell me, what have you got that says he's our man?"

I stared at her. Logically it worked, but in terms of solid evidence, I had nothing. "It has to be him," I said lamely.

"Tell me why."

Everything added up, but I didn't have anything tangible I could hand her or point to. "I guess it's all in how I see it. This man with a down-home way of speaking called on Friday and—"

"He called you?"

"Yes."

"That's it, then. A phone call is evidence. Hold on." She picked up her phone, made a call, and asked for Billy Houseman. Then she said, "Billy, this is Evelyn Hogan. We still lovers, darling?" She grinned as he replied. "I sure do. Please let me know if this number—" she recited the number in my book "—called—" and she gave him my number. "You bet I'll hold. I need it five minutes ago."

It didn't take long. She wrote, smiled, honeyed him a little more, and hung up. "He's our man," she said with satisfaction. "That's my guy at the phone company. Takes less time than going through channels and there's no paperwork. Now, question two. To get a warrant, I have to know what we're going to find in that apartment."

"I don't have the faintest idea. I think he came to New York, stalked her so cleverly she didn't know it, and grabbed her on Thanksgiving Day year before last. He'd already lived in the city for some time. I don't know what he did to her, where he buried her if he killed her—" I really felt kind of dumb, but I knew she was right. Only on television do cops get warrants just by asking for them. In real life they need to know what they expect to find and where they expect to find it. "I suppose he might have kept a memento of his deed, her handbag, her ID."

"Good thinking. Then if they find what's left of the body, it's harder to identify. Good enough. I think we're in business."

"I hope you find him." I said it with mixed emotions. He had the best motive for murder I could think of; he was killing his sister's killer.

"We will. We know who he is now. I suppose you don't walk around with a cellular phone in your bag, so keep in touch with me. I can leave a message for you at home. Meantime, I'm going to call around in Indiana and see what I can find out there."

I left and made my way over to Sixty-fourth Street. Seconds after I rang Olive's bell, a voice came through the intercom asking me who I was. When I responded, the door buzzed open.

Upstairs, a visiting home care worker opened the door for me with a smile and took me to the living room, where Olive sat on the sofa, dressed, her face made up, her hair clean and tidy.

"You look wonderful," I said.

"I feel pretty good. Hospitals don't agree with me. And Amelia here is a big help."

"Are you, as they say, ambulatory?"

"Can I walk? Oh, sure. I'm really feeling pretty good today."

"Suppose we have lunch at the Tavern on the Green."

"The Tavern on the Green," she repeated, almost with wonderment. "I haven't been there for years. Longer than that." She smiled, looking like an older, tougher, thinner version of my mother. "I don't know if I can walk the three blocks or so."

But she hadn't said no. "I'll get a cab to pick us up downstairs and drop us in front of the restaurant."

"That'd be great, Kix."

The cabbie thought we were nuts, but he drove us to the restaurant, which was just inside Central Park three blocks north of the corner where I had first laid eyes on Aunt Olive. We had a table with a view of the park, and Olive ate as though she was very hungry. I guess I was born an optimist, but watching her, talking to her, I knew she had months, maybe years, ahead of her.

We talked about a lot of things, places she had visited—she had spent most of her vacations traveling—people she had run into, known, loved. We never mentioned my mother or my grandparents. When we were finished, after several cups of coffee and sweet desserts, we taxied back to her building and I helped her up to the apartment. She was tired by then, ready to lie down for a nap. She refused my offer of help but thanked me warmly for the lunch and the company. At the door, we hugged each other.

I never saw her again.

28

The call from Detective Hogan came after nine o'clock that night. "Chris? Evelyn Hogan here. We've got him in custody."

My heart did strange things. Since we'd uncovered the body of the real Natalie Miller, I had developed so much sympathy for Ted, her brother, that part of me hoped he would be gone. "Tell me," I said.

"We got the warrant and I had the Borough Task Force detectives waiting when he got home from work. We'd already gotten into his apartment and found what we were looking for."

"Her handbag?"

"Everything of importance that was in it, but he must have trashed the bag itself. Her wallet has a snapshot of her in a wedding dress and her husband next to her."

"It's very sad," I said. "Can I talk to him?"

"Come on down tomorrow."

"What about the other guy?"

"Say, he's something else. 'How ya doin'?' and all that. We picked him up, too, but we don't have enough to hold him. He said he and Miller kind of traded identities when they hooked up in New York, at least so that Miller could get his job."

"Does Miller have a lawyer?"

"The court'll appoint one. He's not what I'd call rich. And he's pretty depressed."

"I'll be down tomorrow afternoon."

I drove down right from the college, munching a tuna fish sandwich as I drove. Evelyn had arranged an interview room for me at the Sixtieth Precinct in Brooklyn as a special favor since I had contributed to the case. I sat down in the empty room and waited only a few minutes. Then the door opened and Steve Carlson, Natalie's friend at Hopkins and Jewell, walked in. He looked pale and tired, his hands cuffed behind him, his hair wild.

"Hi," I said.

"You figured it out."

"It was the phone call that clinched it," I said, "the one your friend made last week. I hadn't given my number to many people and I couldn't believe Martin Jewell had gone looking for Natalie's old apartment house or that Arlene had hired someone to play the brother. It didn't make sense. It had to be someone who had known her and lost track of her. When your friend called, I knew he'd gotten the number from someone and I didn't believe his story that it came from the Indiana newspaper. It was just too far-fetched. Also, it was my husband who called them to place the ad, and he's pretty careful about throwing around our phone number. I figured you'd asked him to call, pretending to be her brother."

"I shouldn't've had him call."

"It would have occurred to me eventually that you had gotten a job with Hopkins in order to befriend the new Natalie. How did you know she worked there?"

"I read my sister's last letter to my mother, but not till a long time after she wrote it. My mother died around the time Natalie was killed. I tried to get hold of her, but she'd moved and left no forwarding address and no new phone number. I wrote and the letter came back. I called and the number'd been disconnected. I had a job up in Alaska and I didn't have time to look for my sister. I had all my mother's things put in storage, and when I came back a couple of years later, I started going through them. There was the letter from Natalie, and she said she'd just been called for an interview at a new ad agency called Hopkins and Jewell."

"She hadn't had the interview yet?"

"Didn't sound like it. So on a chance, I got the number, called, and asked for her. When they put someone on, I said, 'Hi, it's Teddy,' and she said, 'Who?' as though she'd never heard of me. And it wasn't her voice, I mean my sister's voice. It was just too much of a coincidence, my sister getting an interview with this company and someone else with the same name holding a job there. So I took everything I had out of the bank and went to New York."

"You knew she had last lived near Gramercy Park."

"I not only knew it, I'd visited her there when I was in New York almost seven years ago."

"And one morning in the elevator she introduced you to her neighbors, the Fosters."

He looked at me curiously. "You know, you're right. I didn't think to look for anyone in the building. I just asked the super when and where she'd gone. He knew when, but he had no forwarding address. Neither did the post office. And there was no listing in the phone book under her name. I suppose she had an unlisted number, but if she did, that is, the other woman, I couldn't get hold of it. I called a bunch of N. Millers, but they'd never heard of Natalie."

"So you decided to get a job with Hopkins and Jewell," I said.

"I had to learn word processing first, but it wasn't hard. I've learned a lot harder stuff in my life. What was hard was getting a job at H and J. I started out at another place, kind of to hone my skills. Then I found out what employment agency sent people to them. Arlene liked me. She hired me right off."

"Arlene interviewed you herself?"

"After Wormy. They run a pretty tight ship there. One of the partners approved of everyone who was hired."

"So you became Natalie's friend."

"That wasn't easy either. She didn't want boyfriends who weren't rich or promising, and I'm a lot younger than she is. But I managed. We talked a lot and I think she liked me."

"I guess by that time you'd met up with Steve Carlson."

"Yeah. He had no problem lending me his ID. He thought it was a gas. He knew the whole story. He just never knew what I did on Thanksgiving Day."

"Did the fake Natalie ever slip up?"

"Never. She was very cool, always in control. I once asked her where she'd worked before and she was very vague, said it was some place on Sixth Avenue that'd gone out of business. Everything she said was possible. Nothing was checkable."

"You knew where she lived, though, didn't you?"

"She couldn't really keep that a secret. They had her address on file, and Wormy used to distribute a Christmas card list every fall. But she never actually said who she was marrying, not his last name anyway. He was Sandy Somebody and he lived in New Jersey."

"How'd you find her?"

"I followed her a lot and then one day he picked her up. I drove my car to work on a day when they were going out. After that it was easy. And Wormy had her new address after she got married. She needed it for the W Two."

"Did you always intend to kill her?"

"I just wanted to find my sister. I wanted to know what happened to her. I started out thinking maybe this was a coincidence, a second Natalie Miller at H and J, but then I got the feeling there was more to it. I tried to get over it when she left to get married, but I couldn't. I knew I'd only have one chance, that if I let her live, I'd have to get out of town, and I was ready to do that. But I didn't want to burn my bridges. I picked Thanksgiving Day on the chance she'd go to the parade. She'd told me once how much she wanted to go, but no one would take her. So I followed them and waited till one of them might be occupied. She walked around the corner and I gave her a big smile and said hi."

"And she was just as happy to see you."

"Until I grabbed her and ran her through the crowd on Central Park West to the next block. If he went to look for her, she was long gone."

It's very satisfying when everything you know and theorize starts to link up, but this was all so sad, I couldn't take pleasure in the satisfaction. "Did she tell you what she did?"

"When I applied a little pressure."

"Did she tell you why, Ted?"

"I gather they'd both applied for the job at H and J and my sister was called for an interview. The fake Natalie did a little research on her own, went to see what Jewell looked like, and she liked what she saw. She asked my sister to let her go in her place and my sister refused. They went away for a weekend before the interview, she didn't say where, and I guess they had a big fight and my sister ended up dead."

"She didn't tell you where she buried the body?"

He shook his head. "I was desperate to know. She said if I let her go, she'd tell me after she was safe."

"She couldn't have done that," I said. "Your sister was buried on family property. The body would have led right to her killer."

"You found her?"

"On Saturday. The woman posing as your sister was named Connie Moffat. She buried Natalie on her cousin's property that weekend that they went upstate. There was a handbag with the remains and it had Natalie Miller's driver's license in it. And a picture."

"My God."

I pulled Connie's key ring out of my bag.

"That's the key to her desk," he said.

"And this is the key Martin Jewell gave her for the door to the old office when they were having an affair. This one fits the apartment at Gramercy Park." I showed it to him. "What surprised someone I showed it to was how she would have an original key to the apartment on an old key ring if she had to turn it in when she moved. But Connie was a subtenant. She must have given the super her duplicate key from her own key ring without thinking about it. The key she kept was your sister's. There were no keys in the pocketbook."

"She roomed with my sister for a while at the end. They'd met at a class a couple of months before. She told me that on Thanksgiving Day when I was prying information out of her."

"It probably started very innocently."

"I hate that woman," he said with a sob in his throat.

"What did you do with her?" I asked gently.

"Sorry. That's my secret."

"Can I get you anything?"

He shook his head. "Thanks for coming. I led you a merry chase. I didn't expect you to be nice to me."

It hadn't all been kindness. I wanted information from him. I wanted to know the missing details, the motives, the means he had used to achieve his end. "Do you need a lawyer?"

"They read me my rights last night. They'll supply one."

"I can get you someone very good."

He put his head down and wept. I patted him on the back and called for someone to come and let me out.

* * *

I went home and made some phone calls. The first one was to Arnold.

"Haven't heard from you for a while. You get your man yet?"

"Last night. I didn't get him; the police did."

"With a little help from the suburbs."

"A little," I admitted. "It's a very sad case, Arnold."

"Murder is always sad."

"This is a brother avenging his sister's death. I really feel for him."

"You feel for everyone, Chrissie. It's why we love you. I guess he needs a lawyer."

"Very badly. I hate to ask—"

"It sounds like an interesting case. What more can a lawyer ask for?"

Plenty, I thought, but I thanked him and gave him the information he needed. Then I called Sandy Gordon.

29

I had a long talk with Joseph on Wednesday. She called Tuesday evening and said she had a meeting at the Chancery the next morning and could we meet for lunch after that? There was nothing I wanted to do more. My conversation with Sandy had been difficult, to say the least, and I looked forward to sitting down and relaxing with an old friend.

We met at the magnificent restaurant in the Palace Hotel across Madison Avenue from the Chancery at twelve-thirty and Joseph ordered Johnnie Walker Black on the rocks for herself and a glass of Chablis for me. We touched glasses before we sipped.

"I think you have lots to tell me," she said.

"You were right to be concerned about the key. The woman who was kidnapped had murdered a woman named Natalie Miller, and when she buried the body, she removed the dead woman's keys from her handbag. When the killer, Connie Moffat, moved out a few days or weeks later, she must have turned in her own duplicate key and hung on to the dead woman's keys. There were no keys in the dead woman's bag, but there was identification. She was the real Natalie Miller. Connie took on her identity after killing her. They fought about a job, maybe about the man one of them might work for. I'd guess Connie didn't have the kind of work record that the real Natalie had. This was Connie's way of setting her life straight. She started over as someone else."

"And did well in the job, I gather."

"Very well. She worked hard, was dedicated and devoted, managed to have an affair with the boss that unfortunately for her didn't end in marriage. But they went away for a weekend upstate, and while he slept, she drove to the place where she'd buried the real Natalie."

"That was chancey."

"In fact, she got caught. Her cousin was sleeping upstairs and came down with a shotgun to see who was there. They spoke. It was the last time they saw each other."

"You haven't told me who the killer was."

"That's really the saddest part of the story, Joseph. It was the real Natalie's brother."

"A case of revenge."

"Revenge, anger. He wanted to know where her body was buried and she wouldn't tell him. Now he won't say where she's buried."

"Maybe that's his true revenge."

"I gather Connie had a pretty miserable childhood. Her father broke her nose once when he hit her. She must have had it fixed when she came to New York. It's terrible when you see where people are coming from and where they end up. You want to shake them and tell them to give life a chance; violence isn't the way."

"But we're realists."

"Yes."

"And you have another story to tell me."

"I found my mother's sister."

It was a long lunch, and since we were both taking trains from Grand Central, we walked over there together, neither of us in a particular hurry.

I had some errands to run when I got home, and coming back, I spotted Mel out with her kids and they came over to visit. Mel had heard nothing from Sandy, so there was a lot to tell.

By the time she left, I was afraid to call Olive for fear she might be in the middle of an afternoon nap. So I lay down and took one myself.

On Thursday a woman called asking for me. When I said I was Christine Bennett Brooks, she put a man on.

"Mrs. Brooks, this is Stanley Colvin, Olive Cleaver's attorney."

"Is she all right?" I asked, feeling uncomfortable.

"I'm sorry to tell you Ms. Cleaver passed away Monday night."

"Oh no. I saw her Monday. She seemed to be doing so well."

"I think she was very happy to have met you in the last days of her life."

"Would you like me to arrange a funeral?" I felt choked up, but knew the question had to be asked.

"She took care of everything a long time ago, Mrs. Brooks. Her remains were cremated yesterday, and her ashes will be distributed according to her wishes."

"I see."

"She was a very independent person, right up until the end. But she made an addition to her will only a few days before she died. She left you two thousand five hundred dollars and said you would understand why she was giving you that amount."

My tears were falling by that point, but I managed to thank him for calling. My aunt had repaid her debt for all time.

Arnold took over Ted Miller's case. Ted had no desire to stand trial, and Arnold was able to make an interesting deal with the DA. In return for Ted's telling them where the remains of Connie Moffat could be found, the murder charge was reduced to manslaughter. Everyone concerned seemed pretty pleased to have it taken care of that way.

He had killed her and left her body in the Pine Barrens way out on Long Island. He led the police to the spot and they found what was left of Connie Moffat. An autopsy determined she had been shot with a small-caliber gun that Ted no longer owned. Because of the deterioration of the body, it could not determine whether she had been pregnant. But it didn't rule it out.

A few days later Detective Evelyn Hogan called to brief me on some new findings. Connie Moffat had lived in New York for a number of years and held a number of jobs. About ten years earlier she had married, but there was no record of a divorce in New York State, so it was unclear whether her marriage to Sandy was even valid.

Sandy and I met finally to talk. He took me to lunch in New York and apologized for a lot of things he didn't have to apologize for. I gave him back the carton of stuff he had given me so many weeks ago, and the way he looked at it, I had the feeling it was headed for the junk pile.

"I have only one question," I said when the lunch was coming to an end. "Your wedding pictures—you had a Jewish wedding, didn't you?"

"Definitely."

"Did Natalie say she was Jewish?"

"She did, in fact, after she knew I was. I think she must have done a little research before the wedding because she needed her Hebrew name for the papers."

"Interesting."

"And she came up with it when she was asked."

"She really loved you, Sandy."

"I was a fool."

"You're a good-hearted person and you did nothing wrong."

"Thanks, Chris."

He settled our expense account and I refused to take anything for investigating. About a week later I heard that he had sent a very generous donation to the General Superior's fund at St. Stephen's Convent. He couldn't have done better.

I took my inheritance and put it in the bank, where it will accumulate some interest while I think about what to do with it—or forget about it.

Months later, the following November, Jack and I drove into New York early on Thanksgiving Day, parked up near Columbia University, and took a bus down Broadway to Sixty-fourth Street. Then we walked over to Central Park West, passing the Statue of Liberty on the left and Olive's building on the right. On the north corner we stood in the cold and watched the parade. It was everything I remembered and then some, the bands, the horses, the floats, and of course, the huge balloons that floated two stories above us. Jack bought me a balloon and tied it on my wrist, and I laughed a little and cried a little.

I will take my children someday and we will stand on that corner, and while they enjoy the moment, I will remember a time long ago, the happiness of being with my father, and a woman who wanted to make her peace.

Look for these novels by

LEE HARRIS

in your local bookstore.

Published by Fawcett Books.